RETURN TO BLACK FROST ACADEMY

BLACK FROST ACADEMY #2

TATUM RAYNE

Return to Black Frost Academy
Black Frost Academy #2
Copyright © 2023 Tatum Rayne
Published by Hudson Indie Ink
www.hudsonindieink.com

Return to Black Frost Academy/Tatum Rayne - 1st ed. 2023

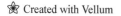 Created with Vellum

PROLOGUE
BO

"Why can't the perverts leave me alone?" My voice snaps like the crack of a whip. My mind is still reeling after the phone call from Mr. Geoffrey. Apparently, the board of trustees would like to have a meeting tomorrow about Frost Enterprises - I don't know how I can make myself any clearer: I. Do. Not. Want. It.

"Calm down." Deacon's deep voice commands.

My body locks up at the tenor of his rumble; the sound rattling his chest from deep within. Tingles start to take over my body as my cheeks heat, and the lust I'm already feeling in his presence taking on a whole new meaning. I try my best to wrangle my libido, to bring it back under my control, as I lift a brow. The smirk that tips the edges of his lips has a small amount of fear washing over me. "I'm sorry," I blurt the words with a huff.

A rumble fills the office as my head whips up, my mouth dries as I find him with his arms folded and a stoic look on his face. "You're sorry, what?" he commands. Another shiver washes over me as my core heats, forcing me to rub my legs together under the desk to try and ease the feeling.

"I'm sorry, Rocket," I smirk as the words pass my lips and I see the muscles in his forearms tense. He growls as I chuckle, his body tensing. "What's the matter Rocket, are you getting pissed with little old me?"

"You know I can't stand that fucking name," he snaps, his tone a harsh crack as a shiver washes over me. I lift a brow, the name on the tip of my tongue.

"Don't be a brat, Bo." he rumbles.

Excitement thrums through me at the desire in his eyes. I know he means it as a threat for some sort of punishment, but honestly, I fucking love it when he goes all Alpha on me. So, do I spend as much time as I can pissing him off? Of course, I do.

"Answer me," he booms – the squeak of the wheels from the office chair splits the air as I jump back away from the desk in surprise.

"I don't know what I'm answering, Rocket?" I purr with a seductive tone. He stalks forward with a determined stride. My eyes widen as I rush to stand.

"Don't even think about it," he orders. The urge to run fills me, but I know it will only be worse if I do. My body feels like a live wire as I watch with bated breath as he rounds the desk and stops behind me. I can feel his warm exhale brush against my ear as the smooth scent of whiskey invades my nose. His solid chest presses into my body from behind. "You know what to do," he whispers into my ear, his voice thickly layered with something that has my core pulsating between my legs.

The urge to do as he's asked is overwhelming, but another part of me wants to defy him to see what happens. It's as if my body is split in two – one side is screaming at me to submit and the other is yelling with all its might to challenge him. Before I can come to a decision a heavy weight presses between my shoulder blades with enough pressure to have me bending over until my left cheek is pressed against the warm wood, with my arse in the air. "Do you want this?" he breathes, with a dark growl, as his hand gently caresses my left globe. Wait, when the hell did he lift my skirt?

"Yes," I whimper as need fills me. The anticipation has my knees feeling weak as the slow torture continues. His hands gently squeeze my arse for a second, before one of his fingers toys with the string of my underwear as he works it out of my ass crack. A snapping sound fills the air as the material hits my skin, the pain has a moan escaping me.

"I don't want to hear any noise as you receive your punishment," he says, as my eyes connect with his over my shoulder. "You know what will happen if you do?"

I bite into my bottom lip feeling the sting of my teeth trying to break the skin. I nod my head in answer as I try my best to shift my weight to relieve some of the pressure between my legs. This is the best and worst feeling ever, how my body responds to all the different things. I try my hardest to ignore the urge to wiggle my arse to try and get this show on the road, but I know he will do as he says, and I'll be left horny as hell. Again.

I'm one big, massive ball of emotion as anticipation mixes with anxiety, lust, and eagerness. He keeps me pressed down on the desk with one hand as the other one tortures me. A cracking sound fills the air, catching me by surprise, as I gasp from the shock. His deep throaty chuckle fills the air as realization dawns on me, and the sting starts to spread through my cheek. I bite my bottom lip harder to stop the moan from escaping, the hurt turns into pleasure and I fight with my knees to keep me in my place.

"Good girl," he purrs as he rubs the area to soothe it with his large hands. "You'll endure ten for being a brat and then if you can keep yourself quiet…" he says. I start to growl in annoyance but quickly manage to stop it before he notices. "We shall see about a reward." Fuck my life. Between them, I'm pretty sure they're trying to *kill* me!

Another crack fills the air, this time on the other cheek and I must force myself to keep quiet. *Two*. The punishment continues as he switches between spanking and soothing the sting. I count to keep myself in the moment and not loose myself to the sensation.

"Ten," he says with a prideful tone as I lay there panting at the sensation overload. Words struggle to formulate in my mind as my legs tremble and the evidence of how turned on I am drips down my thighs. "Bo?"

"Hmm," is the only sound I manage to make as I don't move, my body feeling in a weird, sated state.

"Bo are you ok?" he frets as he pulls me up and my knees give way, so I become a crumpled heap in his arms. My eyes connect with his and seeing the worry on his face has my heart swelling at the love he has for me. I lift a shaky hand, smiling as his eyes narrow – gently, I caress his chin. The stubble rasping against my palm has another round of heat going straight to my centre.

"I'm ok," I manage to say with a throaty rasp as I realize how dehydrated I am. I giggle as I watch him just as intently as he does me. "You really are amazing, you know?"

"Emotional overload," he states with a scoff as I glare daggers at him.

"Don't do that," I chastise as he drops down into the office chair, pulling me into his lap. "Why do you always turn like this after we do anything?" I ask with a curious lilt to my voice. His right hand makes small circles on my back, and I watch as he rubs his eyes with his other hand while blowing out a breath.

Minutes pass us by without a word, as he keeps his eyes closed and rubs his thumb across his chin like he's deep in thought.

"Babe are you happy?" the words burst out of me before I can stop them, as they bring my fears to life. Ever since Frost's funeral and the police confirming to us that my aunt had plans to murder me for the money, he's become more distant. Whereas the others have become overprotective and not allowing me a moment to myself, he has been more silent than usual, and that bothers me.

"Of course, I'm happy. Why would you say that?" he demands as he glowers at me, pulling me closer so his head is resting on top of mine.

"I know you've always been the silent type, but I feel like you're pulling away from us," I admit. I try to swallow the saliva, but my throat feels like razor blades have shredded it from the admission.

"I'm sorry," he says, his tone filled with a tiredness I've never noticed before. "Honestly, I'm worried." I pull my head free from under his, forcing him to release the hold he has on me so I can see his eyes. That's when I notice the dark circles, like he's not slept in days.

"I've got a bad feeling," he states. My heart starts to beat erratically at the look in his eyes.

What more could go wrong?

CHAPTER ONE

A nervous energy pulsates under my skin as my palms become slick with sweat. I run my hands over the lapels of the blazer once more as I try to smooth out imaginary creases. "Take a deep breath, Bo," Mr. Geoffrey says from his seat. I lift a brow as I continue to fuss over myself. How can he sit there so calm and collected when we have to meet the men who're about to try and tear me to pieces? I don't get how he can look so chill about all this.

"You're not the one about to face the firing squad, are you?" I sass, as my mood becomes increasingly hostile with each passing minute.

"Neither are you," he shoots back with a blank expression. I scoff, as I stare out of the huge floor to ceiling windows at the town. My entire body feels jittery as the wait continues. I look at my watch to check the time. My teeth grind together as I realize we've been out here for fifteen minutes. Do they not know I have other shit I need to do today?

"They're ready for you," a bright cheery voice says. I spin around as Mr. Geoffrey stands to find the petite young blonde from the foyer smiling at us. I inhale deeply filling my lungs, as much as I can, as I straighten my shoulders. *"You're Bo fucking Walker, you don't cower in anybody's presence. So, straighten your crown, bitch, and show them exactly how English girls rule the boardroom."* The inner pep talk does wonders, and with my head held high I walk past them and into the meeting room. The doors shut behind us with a soft click as all the heads whip around to face us.

"Ah, Miss Walker, so good of you to join us today." I nod my head in acknowledgement, as I stride to the head of the table and take a seat, fighting the smirk as all the eyes in the room widen.

"Gentlemen," I say with a sharp snap to my tone. "I understand you're wanting to discuss the problem you have with me not wanting the company." I say, as I flick my eyes between each of the men, making sure our eyes connect for a second. "But you will not change my mind."

"Watch who you're talking to, girl," a burly voice says. My head snaps to my right connecting with a younger man sandwiched between two of the older men. "Some very disturbing things have come to light."

"How so?" I muse as I look to Mr. Geoffrey who sits on my left with zero emotion on his face. I know it's for the people in the room.

"Frost Enterprises is at a critical level since the unfortunate demise of the CEO," the burly man says. His words make a lump form in my throat, as memories flash to the front of my mind. *Son of a bitch.*

"Unfortunate demise of a psychopath and rapist?" I growl.

All but two of the seven men surrounding the table shuffle uncomfortably in their seats. I've been hounded by the press since that day, all of whom have accused me of all sorts of things. "Bo," Mr. Geoffrey hisses at me, to remind me to keep my cool and not tear into this insufferable arsehole.

"I don't know how I can make my feelings any clearer," my tone is clipped. "I do not want anything to do with Frost Enterprises. So, either liquidate it, auction it off, or whatever." Chatter breaks out throughout the room as all the men start to talk at once.

"Miss Walker?" a voice says somewhere in the buzz of the chaos. However, I can't work out who is speaking. "Miss Walker, please?"

"Silence!" My command booms throughout the room, shutting them all up instantly. I look to each man and my stomach rolls as I get a good look at them for the first time. I recognize three of them from the society.

"Miss Walker?" a croaky voice says once again as an older man stands at the far end of the table. "We've asked you here because we are in need of a loan to keep the company in business." Excuse me – you are fucking what now? Are they blatantly choosing to ignore everything I have said in the last two months? Are they all medicated, and it has stopped working or some shit? That's got to be it.

"Gentlemen," Mr. Geoffrey says as he stands. "Miss Walker has made it very clear she doesn't want anything to do with the company and as she is the only Frost left, it is her right to do as she sees fit." Thank God for this man. He has been my saving grace over the last two months as I've tried my best to deal with everything emotionally, and to guide me with all I have received from my family and Frost.

"She isn't a Frost," a voice snaps out. The burly man stands and thumps his fist on the table. All the other men in the room cower away from him.

"Delaney, we all know you have a problem with her because of her aunt. But now is not the time or place to air out your dirty laundry." Mr. Geoffrey has the room rearing back in shock at his words. Clearly, they're not used to someone calling them out on their shit.

"I'm glad that bitch is dead," he says with a savage smile. "But that has nothing to do with this." His eyes narrow on me and all I see reflected in them is hatred. "She isn't a Frost," he repeats.

"I think…" Mr. Geoffrey begins when the man rudely cuts him off with another sadistic smile.

"They were never married."

"How dare you!" My voice booms as I push to my feet, glaring at him. "You and two others were witness to the wedding and everything that followed it." I snarl, as the other men in the room look between each other in confusion. "For the few of you that weren't there, and maybe not part of this so-called *society*, Delaney here, plus him, and him," as I point to the offenders "watched while we consummated the marriage with an audience." Shocked gasps fill the air as I continue to have a stare down with Delaney.

"Here," he says with a smirk as he slides a file across the table. Mr. Geoffrey intercepts it, he opens it up reading the first page when he grumbles. Delaney the ass hasn't broken eye contact with me yet, and I sure as hell am not going to be the one who gives in first.

"Bo?" The tremble of the voice has me looking away from the arsehole. My gaze connects with Mr. Geoffrey's, finding horror reflected in his eyes. He shakily passes me the paper, my anxiety spikes as the room goes deathly silent - you could hear a pin drop.

My eyes scan the paperwork as my mind races to process what it means, the room starts to spin as my breathing becomes labored. My head snaps up, Mr. Geoffrey drops his chin in a small nod confirming it's true. The paperwork in my hand is a contract between Frost's father and a Mason Novack. It declares him as the officiant at the wedding where Frost would marry me under false pretenses, so his father could gain access to my inheritance. Mr. Novack would receive a tidy sum for the act he played in it.

The paper creases in my hand. "Why am I here?" I demand as I try to keep my emotions under wraps. Honestly, I don't have a clue what I'm feeling right now at this revelation.

"As you are the Queen of the town and the wealthiest person, we would like to come to some sort of a deal so we can keep the business going," another of the men says.

"No," I snap as drop the file on the desk with a thwack and move away like it's riddled with poison.

"No?" he demands. My brow lifts as our eyes meet and I can see his body giving away the telltale signs of nervousness. He shifts from foot-to-foot as his hands run down the front of his heavily pressed suit.

"Mr. Delaney, you clearly want this business. Whether it be to go head-to-head with me or to try and take control of the town, the latter of which I think is more likely," I say with a strong emotionless tone. "No, I will not give you anything of mine. Now, have a good day, gentlemen." I snap as I stride out of the room. Shouts for me to stop hit my retreating back. If they think I'm going to sit there for another moment after that bombshell; well, let's just say they'll have more chance of getting blood out of a stone.

Mr. Geoffrey follows closely behind on my heels as we continue through the corridor to the elevator. "Miss Walker, stop!" a voice booms behind us and I pay it no mind as the doors open with a ping. We step inside and the button lights up as one of the older men rushes towards us. "I would like to talk to you," he says.

"Have a good day," are my last words as the doors slide closed.

"Well, that was eventful." I try to hold back the giggle as we both look at each other with smirks on our faces. "How was my performance, Mr. Geoffrey?" I ask with a grimace on my face.

"Oscar worthy," he says with a genuine smile. I may seem like a heartless bitch at the moment, but I found out about the fake wedding two weeks ago and I've been trying to wrap my head around it ever since. The guys know something is bothering me, but I haven't plucked up the courage to tell them the truth, yet. Now, I've played the part of the confused girl because I know all the men in that room are after my crown.

"You do know they will come after you when everything is revealed?" The worried tone has me looking to Mr. Geoffrey. I give him a soft smile to try and comfort him.

"I know they will, and I think that Delaney and Weinstein are working together," I muse as I massage my left temple as tension pounds in the area, making it feel like my head has its own heartbeat. Ugh, great now I'm going to have the mother of all headaches.

"You really think so?" The look on his face is halfway between shock and confusion.

"Yeah, he's been very vocal since the funeral, demanding meetings with me." The first time around I did meet with him, but that was cut short when he started demanding I pay for his daughter's tuition. He thought I owed the pair of them that much for ruining their lives, because apparently the deal was set for her to become Frost's wife and I screwed it up.

The elevator doors slide open. We step out and I glance around. *Where is everyone?* The foyer is normally a bustle of activity, but there is nobody around. Only the two people, that we saw when we came in - a security guard sits behind the reception desk and a woman sits to his left. A couple of people walk through with what looks to be expensive suits, but that's it. We cross the foyer quick time, pushing through the doors out onto the street, where I stop and take a much-needed inhale of fresh air, the cool crisp feeling of it helps settle the anxiety I've had since this morning

Mr. Geoffrey doesn't wait with me as he goes to stand near the car that's already at the curb. He knows I need a few minutes to myself after that meeting. I still can't wrap my head around how I'm an eighteen-year-old with a huge fortune and businesses. I made sure someone is acting as CEO, on my behalf, but also making sure all final decisions come through me. I never thought my life would be like this when I was in England. Was my life perfect there? No. Did we struggle a lot of the time? Yes, we did. Would I have changed it for this? Hell fucking no. Money doesn't buy you happiness, and the people that say it does are only kidding themselves.

The street is filled with people rushing around, while either tapping away on their phones or on calls. How can a self-sufficient town run like it's a major city and not a single person from the outside world realize this place is here? I gasp as my eyes land on a person standing on the opposite side of the street, staring at me as people rush around him. It can't be? Rubbing the heel of my palms into my eyes, I look again, but the spot where I saw him is now empty. My chest tightens as emotion washes over me like a tidal wave. I rush towards the car, making Mr. Geoffrey stand to attention. "Did you see him?" I blurt the words as my chest becomes heavier.

"Who?" he asks as he whips around in a circle, a look of confusion on his face as he faces me again.

"Frost. He was standing right there," I demand as I point to the spot I've just seen him.

"Bo, sweetie, he's dead," he says with a soft voice, a pained expression washes over his features as his brows furrow.

"I saw him, Mr. Geoffrey. He was standing right there!" I

plead with him to believe me, his hands land on my shoulders – squeezing them, as he watches me intently with a sad look on his face. My hands tremble as I play the situation over in my mind. I did see him. He was there. I know he was. But why was he just watching, why didn't he come over to speak to me?

"Bo. We buried him two months ago, you've obviously seen someone who looks like him," he says again with a tone like he's speaking to a small child. The pain in my head throbs harder this time, making me wince.

"Yeah," I reply, as I crane my neck to look for him, again. "The migraine must be messing with me."

CHAPTER TWO

"Hey, Beautiful, how was the meeting?" Rafe asks as I walk into the kitchen. My head is killing me. I pull out a glass from the cabinet as I flick the tap on and fill it half full. My bag hits the marble surface with a thud as I rummage through it looking for my painkillers. I find them, pushing two out of the pack. Throwing them down my throat instantly, as I gulp down the water to swallow, my eyes connect with a worried looking Rafe over the rim of the glass. "Bo, what's going on?"

"Mr. Geoffrey thinks I'm going crazy," I blurt just as he walks into the kitchen. He throws his hands up in defense as a pissed off looking Rafe spins to face him.

"Bo, you know it's not possible what you're saying" he replies not taking his eyes off Rafe.

"I'm telling you. I saw him standing there!" I boom, slamming the glass down into the sink. I stride out of the kitchen without a word to either of them. I make it halfway up the stairs. "Rafe, I need to talk to you and the others."

I don't hear his reply as I stomp the rest of the way to my room, which was a mistake as the migraine has taken on a life of its own now. I burst through the door, and a scream fills the air, making me wince and rub my head. Ms. Jeanette stands there with wide eyes and a hand to her chest. "Jesus child. You scared the life out of me," she says. I mumble my apology as I pull the blazer off, while kicking my shoes off at the same time. I walk over and crawl across the bed not bothering to pull back the covers. I faceplant on the pillow, groaning as the softness of it swallows me like a cocoon.

"Everything ok, child?" she asks as I feel the bed dip at the side of me. With a huff I turn my head slightly, keeping my eyes closed to try and stave off the bright light.

"Mr. Geoffrey thinks I'm going mental," I say with a defeated tone. I can kind of see his point of why it's not possible, but he was standing right there!

"Why would he think that?" With a huff, I roll off the bed and close the shutters, which gives me some peace from my pounding head.

"After the meeting I just needed a few minutes to breathe in the air and centre myself." She nods her head, like she knows how that feels. "Someone was watching me from the opposite side of the road." I say with a shrug. The look of concern on her face has me wishing I hadn't opened my mouth, but I know she won't judge me as quickly as Mr. Geoffrey did.

"Ok. That doesn't seem like a reason for Mr. Geoffrey to think you're going crazy."

"It was Frost," I admit, as I drop down onto the bed and cross my legs.

"Frost?" she gasps with wide eyes. "Child you…"

"Yeah, I know it's not possible. But honestly, he looked just like him." My eyes connect with hers, hoping to find understanding on her face. But what I find, instead, is worry and sadness. Thinking about it now, I can see why they think I'm losing the plot, but he was right there. Dammit! I throw the pillow off the bed with enough force it ends up on the sectional. Ms. Jeanette looks shocked at my outburst but doesn't say anything further.

"I'm sorry," I croak the words as I feel my eyes begin to pool with tears. "I think I'm tired and everything is getting on top of me."

"Sleep child. It will do you a world of good," she says with a soft smile on her face. I pull back the covers and wiggle my way underneath them so I'm comfy. I smile at her as I feel my lids become heavy with sleep.

"Thank you for sticking with me," I mumble, as I feel the exhaustion take over.

"I'll always be here for you."

"Please don't do this," I hear myself say between sobs. Oh god no! Please stop. I hear his palm connect with my face. I can't bring myself to open my eyes and watch that day as if I was a bystander. I hear sneered words, but I can't make them out.

"Bo?" The tone has me opening my eyes and I can see the tears on his face. "Bo, look at me," he commands my other self and I find myself staring at him and only him.

"I'm so sorry, baby." His tone sounds defeated, and my chest deflates. As I watch the horror on his face as he tries to free himself.

"I wonder if you're going to feel as sweet as I imagine." I close my eyes, begging with my sleep state to let me wake up. The dream doesn't disappear as I continue to beg with everything that I am. It's like the dream wants to keep me here to torture me.

"Are you ready for a real man, girl?" My body starts to

17

tremble, as I watch through blurred vision how terrified I am and how desperate he is to try and help me.

"Switch off. Be anywhere but here," Frost commands. The tears are now streaming down my face as I see the guilt written on his face. The dream shifts.

"Today we are gathered here to remember a troubled young man, who left this world too soon." The words fill me with horror. No. No. No. I can't relive this again! I can't. I scream at myself to wake up, but nothing happens as I watch myself staring and immobile.

"Babe, it's ok," I hear Knox coo, as he pulls me closer to his side.

"I should have been the one lying there," I mumble. Seeing the look on my face has the tears rolling like a river as I try and watch the worst day of my life. I'm barely managing to stop myself from being swallowed whole by the guilt.

"Listen to me," Deacon growls behind me. "He did what he had to do to make sure you got out of there alive. I know we had our differences at the end, but Frost wouldn't have forgiven himself if he had survived and you hadn't." Even now, hearing his words, they still don't give me any comfort.

They didn't see the guilt on his face as he realized his father was my stalker, or how he begged me to keep my eyes on him so I wouldn't have to see whatever his father was planning on doing to me. The hopelessness I could see when he realized he couldn't get free.

I watch as my other self's body moves on its own, like I'm being pulled forward by an invisible wire. The guys grab at me as I move closer to the coffin. I pick up the one black rose, the only one amongst the white ones. I bring it to my lips and kiss the petals before watching it drop into the hole. It lands on top of the plaque with his name carved into the gold, my legs give way beneath me as I hit the ground sobbing. I look down at the coffin as I lay on the floor sobbing; as my heart breaks all over again at seeing this. The rain begins to fall, and I lift my chin to allow it to hit my face, as I try to figure out why this is happening. I've never experienced a dream like this before.

"It's not your fault, Majesty," I hear Axel say to my other self.

"I knew deep down you always loved me." I spin around so fast I almost slip into the hole.

"What the fuck?"

"How you doing, Bo - Bo?" My limbs tremble as I stare at Frost, as he stands in front of me with a sheepish smile on his face.

"What the?" I look between my other self and the guys and the hole, as the coffin finishes its descent. A deep raspy chuckle leaves him as my head swings back and forth. You're imagining this.

"I thought you would be happier to see me, since you're the one who brought me here," he says with a smirk. I look him over. He looks the same, but different in another way as he stands with his hands in his jean pockets and his hair a mess.

"How?" I mumble as my hands start to tremble at seeing him standing here.

"Your guilt."

My subconscious is a real bitch if she thinks this is funny. How many more ways do I have to be tortured? This is all a dream. Nothing here is real, apart from the memory and the emotions that feel like they're clawing me to shreds from the inside out. I close my eyes and slowly count to ten, taking deep breaths through my nose and exhaling through my mouth. You're dreaming. You can wake yourself up. Wake up. C'mon wake the fuck up! I scream at myself.

"I'm sorry." My eyes snap open and they connect with his blue ones. I gasp at how close he is, as I stumble back in

19

surprise. He grasps me gently by the elbow, pulling me away from the edge of the hole. My lower lip begins to shake as my eyes pool with unshed tears and I drop my head.

"Why are you sorry?" I whisper, the guilt rolling in my stomach like it's a living being – just waiting so it can consume me from the inside out. "I'm the reason you're dead."

"Don't do that." He commands as he grabs my chin between his fingers, pulling my head back up to look at him. "Don't blame yourself for the shitshow that was my life, babe." I open my mouth to answer but words fail me as his hand covers my mouth to stop me. "Just listen for once in your life and don't fight me on this," he demands. Silence surrounds us for second. A slow smile spreads across his face at my silence.

"Good girl," he purrs. "You're not to blame for anything and I want you to stop. I was the idiot who fucked us both up because I couldn't get over myself and admit what I really wanted from the beginning," he says with a thick layer of emotion in his voice. "I know you hated me for what I did. But when my father took you, that was it for me – I knew I had to save you one way or another."

His shoulders slump, the tears fall as he rests his forehead against mine. "It was the only way I could make amends for everything. I just wish I did it sooner – then, maybe I could've made you love me as much as I love you."

"Frost." The words break free on a sob.

"I haven't finished," he chastises. "I should've protected you, instead of hurting you. You'll never know how much that guts me to realize. But I have always loved you in my own twisted version of love. I do need you to do one thing for me babe."

"What?" I croak as hug him willingly for the first time, my emotions coming to the surface. "Love the guys with everything

that you are. Things will get harder now that you're who you truly are meant to be." He says pulling me closer into him, his scent fills my nose as I bury my head into his chest. "You were right what you said that day. A queen can take a king and you did. Be the queen you are and don't let anyone crumble your empire."

A cold shiver washes over me as I fall forward. "Frost!" I shout as my eyes snap open finding me alone in the cemetery. "Frost, where are you?" I scream as my head whips back and forth searching for him.

"You will always be our queen." His words moved along with the breeze, carrying them on the journey it takes. I collapse onto the ground sobbing as it dies down and I'm left alone in this place.

"Frost!" I scream as I launch forward. Pain radiates through my head as a grunt has me opening my eyes. I feel the wetness on my cheeks as tears continue to stream down my face. "Shhh," a voice coos as someone pulls me into their side. I can make out that Axel is the one holding me. "H-He." My words break off with a sob, as Frost's words from the dream filter through my mind. "He was there with me," I say the words between sobs as I feel the mattress dip all over.

"Who was?" Deacon asks from my other side with a concerned look on his face.

"Frost," I say with a trembling admission. All their eyes widen as they look to one another, worry etched on their faces. No one says a word, as the cool air in the room begins to seep into my bones, now that the heat has worn off from the dream. I look down at the covers in confusion as realize how disheveled the covers are. I must have been thrashing around badly. I look around the room and see all the guys in boxers, they must have either been on their way to bed or in here with me as the dream took hold.

"You're exhausted babe. You need to sleep," Rafe says as he rubs my feet from the bottom of the bed. "I can't. I can't go through reliving what happened. It's too much," I plead with him. I can't keep going through that again. The bedroom door swings open, and Ms. Jeanette waddles through the room with a cup in her hands. The smile disappears as she takes in all the bleak looks in the room.

"What's wrong child?" she asks as she tries to speed up.

"What's that?" Deacon asks.

"Valerian and chamomile tea I got from my friend. I thought it might help Bo. She says it helps with sleep." She passes the cup to me, and I breathe in the smell. I'm surprised it doesn't have a weird smell to it. "Drink child," she says.

I blow gently on the warm drink as the ceramic cup heats my palms. Cautiously I pull it to my lips and take a small sip. Huh? It's not as hot as I thought it would be, and the taste is nicer than I thought as I take a healthy gulp this, which gains me a wide smile from her. The guys all have slight smiles on their faces, as I drain the last of the contents. My limbs start to feel heavy as a yawn escapes me, Axel gently lays me down. Pulling the covers up to my chin, tucking me in as he drops a kiss on my forehead. I feel the oblivion that I was so savagely pulled out of calling me back and I give into it as the tea Ms. Jeanette gave me takes effect. Just as I'm swallowed whole, I hear "Kitchen now. We all need to talk."

CHAPTER THREE

AXEL

"What's…" I glower at Rafe to shut him up, as I close the door on a soft snoring Bo. The guys have really been pissing me off recently. I've tried to tell them that she's been spiraling for days but they wouldn't believe me. Saying "Oh no, she's fine. There's nothing to worry about." Now she's telling us she's seeing him, and they aren't worried? Yeah, right. Ms. Jeanette is glaring at us all as we make our way down the corridor and descend the stairs.

"Why are you forcing us all to have a talk in the kitchen?" Knox grouches, my upper lip pulls back in a snarl at the childish behavior.

"Because boy, he's as worried as I am." Ms. Jeanette snaps as she takes a seat at the island.

All their heads shoot to her with wide eyes. I shake my head slowly at how dense they're truly being. "What are you talking about?" Rafe grumbles with a sour look on his face.

"Are y'all seriously that blind?" She snaps, her brows pinch together, and so does her mouth, making her look like she's chewing on a lemon. "Y'all have been more concerned with her spending time with you equally than you are about noticing her wellbeing."

"She's spiraling out of control. Imagining she sees Frost when she's out." Guilt punches me in the gut again. Why did it take me so long to see she was hurting? The guys become unnaturally quiet, which, for themselves, is a dead giveaway the feeling has hit home for them too. "You all need to do better for her. Because I made a promise to protect that girl!" her voice booms in the kitchen. "Do not make me look a fool."

I watch wide eyed as she storms out of the kitchen. All our heads turn and watch her as she goes. My head slowly turns back to the others, seeing a range of emotions across their faces. "How didn't I see what was going on?" Deacon muses as he rubs his chin.

"It's not your fault."

"I should've known!" He roars, the sound of the stool screeching along the floor, and joining in the chorus of his tone. "She's been coming to my room more. Pleading with me to make her feel something else."

"Axel?" Knox's voice grabs my attention. I lift a brow at him. "What have you seen?" he asks.

"She's not right and she hasn't been for a long time to be honest," I say with a feeling of someone punching a hole through my chest. "But you know Majesty. She won't open up about her emotions." Rumbles of agreement fill the room. We all know how she is and love her for it, but this isn't helping. Screams fill the air, the sound is filled with so much pain and anguish my knees nearly buckle.

"I've got her," I shout over my shoulder as I take off up the stairs and down the corridor. My hands tremble as I grab the handle. Another scream fills the air, but this time it's filled with so much anguish my heart feels like its dropped into my feet. I hear his name, like the passing of the breeze, as she goes quiet once more.

Taking a deep breathe, I open the door and make my way inside. The covers are in a mass on the floor as she lays there. Looking like she's in a tranquil sleep and nothing can disturb her, I hear murmurs, but nothing that is loud enough for me to hear. When she bolts upright screaming his name again, as the tears stream down her face, I rush forward, dropping down on the bed behind her. Pulling her back into my chest to try and comfort her. "I'm here Majesty," I say with a featherlight whisper into her ear. "I got you."

Her whimpers gut me, as she wriggles herself closer to me like she's trying to become one with me. I lay back with her in my arms, pulling her closer so I can drop a kiss on her forehead. Relief floods me as I see her terror from the nightmare she's having start to settle. A soft exhale leaves her as she snuggles in closer and I feel her body continue to relax, I get myself comfortable, making sure I have a tight hold. I listen intently as her breathing deepens and wait with bated breath to see if she starts thrashing again. I feel myself begin to doze off, and worry fills me, my mind buzzing – I love this girl so much, but seeing her like this brings me to my knees every time.

"Dude?" the voice pulls me out of the fog as exhaustion sweeps over me. My head snaps to the right to find Rafe stood at the side of the bed.

"She, ok?" he asks with a sorrowful look on his face. I nod my head as I look down at the sleeping beauty in my arms. Her long blonde hair billows across the pillow like a halo and tans I hear her soft, content breaths.

"Yeah, I think so," I say with a whisper as I try to adjust myself to get the feeling back in my arm, which is numb. "I think everything is just too much for her at the moment. But as soon as I pulled her into me, she settled."

"Really?" he says as he watches her as intently as I am.

"Yeah. She doesn't sleep alone from now on."

"Agreed," he says with a confident nod of his head.

"What have you guys been talking about since I've been up here?"

I watch as the set of his shoulders deflates and his brows crease. Clearly, he's not happy with the conversation. He rubs his thumb along his bottom lip slowly, and I find my eyes tracking the movement fascinated by it. *What the fuck are you doing? Stop it!* I divert my eyes looking down at the girl in my arms. "Are we going to talk about what happened?"

"Can you stay with her?" I ask as I gently slide my arm free, climbing to my feet. I come face to face with him, and I see the pleading look up close. I shake my head and move past him, making my way towards the bathroom. I close my eyes as I breathe through my noise, while trying to calm my nerves.

"Don't walk away from me," Rafe growls behind me, the sound loud in the room – I cut him a glare and look behind him at the girl still asleep.

"It happened. I thought we agreed she was our main concern?" I throw back, turning my attention back to what I'm doing.

"Don't do that, Axel," he pleads with me.

I wasn't confused or anything, after me and Rafe had sex after the funeral, but what I don't like is that we've kept it a secret. I don't feel ashamed of who I am, but I can switch so quickly between a man and woman that it's never been something I've had to think about. Now, I have to consider another person's feelings about things, but Majesty is something else to me entirely, and I don't want this upsetting her. Also, I'm not really sure how the others will take it because I'm almost certain they don't know about Rafe either.

"We agreed that she was our one, but I can't deny what happened between us either," he says softly.

"Dammit, Rafe," I whisper shout as I tuck myself back into my jeans. I spin around to face him, wincing as our foreheads connect because he's standing so close. Our noses touch, as his scent invades my nose making my mouth water. "Do they even know about you?" I ask bluntly. Guilt consumes me as I see the smile drop off his face and his shoulders curl over.

"I think they've had an idea, but they've never asked. I've also done what I needed to do to keep it away from the gossip at the school," he says. Seeing the expression on his face, has me twining our fingers together to try and comfort him.

"What about Bo?" I ask with a curious lilt to my voice.

"You really think she would think differently of us?" he asks with sheer panic on his face.

"No, I don't think she would. But we need to decide what we're doing before anything else." I say with pursed lips. "I know you love her as much as I do, but we need to approach this carefully, because I can't lose her."

His eyes widen as I see the terror take over him. I know now he's terrified of what she and the others will think. My heart drops, knowing I'll never truly have what I want. My lips claim his brutally, I'm shocked how quickly things turned, but I don't regret it as Rafe moans into my mouth. I nip his bottom lip with my teeth, pulling a gasp from him so he opens up to me, allowing me to caress his tongue with my own, making a perfect erotic dance of our own. I grip the back of his neck harder, yanking his head back as I break the kiss with a wet smack.

Lust-filled eyes stare at me and I smirk devilishly at him, as I run my tongue across his stubbled jaw. Paving a wet track down his throat and around to the side of his neck where I nip his skin, with a dark chuckle, as he moans louder. Another moan echoes along with ours, driving us to jump apart. Both our heads snap to the door with labored breathing, as my eyes widen, finding Bo leaning against the door frame as she rubs her legs together.

"Don't stop on my account," she grins as her lust-filled gaze flicks between the pair of us. Rafe's face is bright red, as he stares wide-eyed at her. I can see my reflection out of my peripheral and I can see the blush creeping up my face. Rafe takes off like a bat out of hell, rushing through the door, leaving Bo and I here with confused looks on our faces.

"Shit. Axel, I'm sorry," she says, grinding her toes into the floor with a sheepish look on her face.

"I guess you know now," I say through gritted teeth. I should've stayed away and this shit wouldn't be happening – my heart pounds in my chest as I watch her watching me.

"I've always known."

I start to cough as confusion fills me, and I feel like I'm choking on my own saliva. My heart rate picks up feeling like I've got a train racing through there. "How?" I croak between coughs, she giggles as she walks over. Her arms engulfing me in a hug, my veins buzz because of the connection. I thought she would have turned away after seeing us.

"I've known you like each other for months now, and then I saw you together in the office."

My mouth drops open as she smiles. "We want you," I blurt the words in a panic, the look on her face doesn't give me anything and that terrifies the life out of me. She was the thing that I never saw coming and I can't lose it. I saw how much Frost fucked her up - how she fought her feelings for him, and he did the same thing.

"I want all of you," she says. "I've been dying to ask you both to fuck each other while we've been together, because it really turns me on."

"Majesty, honestly, it just happened," I blurt, rushing through my words, feeling the urge to explain myself – to make her see that it wasn't a betrayal, but that I want him, too.

"It's ok," she smiles softly." But I want to know who I can peg first?" My eyes open so wide with shock I can't believe my eyeballs aren't rolling across the floor. "Ha-ha! Lighten up, babe, I need to go and talk to Rafe," she says as she walks away leaving me with my mouth hanging on the floor.

CHAPTER FOUR

BO

"Rafe?" I say sheepishly as I knock on the door frame, I find him sitting on the bed with his head in his hands. Seeing him like this has a wave of protectiveness washing over me, and I walk over, taking a seat next to him. But how do I protect him from the pain I caused? Me and my damn mouth. The whispered shouts woke me from the shitty sleep I was in. I was worried so I went to see what was going on and I found them kissing like they needed air and I was lost to the lust.

"I'm so sorry," he says. I can clearly see the guilt he feels but he really shouldn't. I'm so glad it happened, and I was the one that laid the foundation for it to happen – guilt fills me at how guilty they both feel because of me.

"You don't need to be sorry, Rafe. I was the one who told you to fuck him," I admit on a sheepish breath.

"What?" he gasps as he lurches to his feet with enough force to nearly topple me off the bed. His hands run through his hair as he paces, his eyes finally meeting mine. I nod my head to confirm I wasn't lying, and that I was the one to push them into it. I just want my boys to be as happy as they make me.

"I'm sorry," I say as he sits back down, and I take his hands in mine and rest them on my lap. "I knew there was something going on," I begin to say, I watch stunned as his mouth opens to say something making me hold a finger up to stop him. "I know it's nothing like you cheating on me. I was the one who egged you both on that night when we were all drunk."

"What do you mean?" he asks, his features pinched, as I see the confusion on his face.

"I've watched you all for a long time and realized you were never truly happy with women constantly in and out of your bed. But I also saw the look in your eyes every time we fuck together." They look at each other the way they look at me, that's why I knew I had to push them together.

"Were we that obvious?" he asks like he's horrified which really pisses me off.

"No, you weren't but I do know you both better than you know yourselves." I smile sweetly at him. "I've been dying to ask you both to fuck for ages because it turns me on so much. The atmosphere between you both was so thick with lust it affected me every time, as well. So selfishly I did it for me, too."

"You?" he asks with raised eyebrows, like he can't believe the words that have just passed my lips.

"Yeah, I've had a few fantasies." I break off with a coy smile as I build up the courage to say what I need to. "I've seen the way you both gravitate to each other and how you're happy when we are all together but when it is just the three of us – you shine. That makes it better for me in every way, " I bite my lip trying to stop a chuckle at the confused look on his face.

"It doesn't mean I want to be with him and not you," he blurts, his hands begin to tremble as I see the panic set in. I grab his face pulling him close until our breaths combine. My eyes search his to try and work out what is going on in his mind.

"Rafe, I love you and I know you love me, too," I begin to say.

"But…"

"Shhh," my index finger presses against his lips to keep him quiet. "I know you feel like you've betrayed me, but you haven't. If anything, I betrayed you both by setting this up. It hurt me to see the way you were denying yourselves to make me happy." I break eye contact, my eyes landing on our entwined fingers on my lap as my chin starts to tremble and the prickle behind my eyes starts.

"Hey," a deep gruff voice fills the room. I don't have lift my head because I already know who it is. He clearly couldn't do with waiting around to find out what was happening. "Majesty you, ok?" he asks closer this time.

Rafe pulls me onto his lap as he cocoons me in his strong arms – I blow out a harsh breath. Why the fuck am I nearly crying when I was the one who did this? I lift my head and instantly find both of their concerned eyes on me.

"I know I set you both up, but the guilt you are feeling is making me emotional because you both shouldn't be feeling like this. I was the one who pushed you together and the guilt is tearing me apart inside because I don't want to hurt either of you."

"I heard everything you said to Rafe," my eyes widen as I stare at him, his cheeks tinge pink as he looks between us both sheepishly.

"You what?" Rafe asks from over my shoulder, his hand hasn't stopped the slow circles he's been rubbing on my back.

"I was stuck to the wall, so you didn't see me," he says with a shrug of his shoulders, like him listening in wasn't a douche thing to do. "I want you both and honestly I'm happy Majesty did what she did, but now I want to know where do we all go from here?" I twist round to face Rafe, smiling a little as he gasps and narrows his eyes at me.

"What do you want?" his eyes drop like he's too shy to say what he truly wants and that hurts my heart.

"I want you both to be completely happy and if that's together, then…" I start to say. Rafe's head snaps up to mine and I give him a sweet smile to try and reassure him that it's ok.

"I want you both," he blurts the words. "I love it when we're all together and I want it to be us."

"Rafe, I love the others too," I say in panic, my heart is pounding as my brain rushes to work out what he means. I can't choose between them – I can't. It would break me more than it did with Frost.

"No, I mean I want all of us as one." Both Axel and I lift a brow in question. "Shit!" Rafe barks as he takes a deep breath. "What I mean is, I want you both as one." I think I kind of know what he means but my brain is taking forever to put all the pieces together.

"I'm confused," I say with a small voice, because for some reason my brain is telling me that this is the end for us.

"I don't want to be with you both separately," he says. My chest collapses with a relieved breath. "I want it to be us when we are together, all three of us. I don't love either of you any less than the other."

"Together?" Axel enquires, with a voice thick with some sort of emotion, his eyes bouncing between the pair of us.

"Yes. Together. We do everything together instead of separately and we do what comes naturally when we…" The smile on Rafe's face is huge as my mind finally catches up to what he's saying. A girly squeak passes my lips as I launch myself at him with enough force to topple us both in a pile on top of the bed. A crushing weight presses onto my back as a deep rumble of laughter fills the room. Rafe cusses up a storm below me which has me laughing my arse off at the annoyed look on his face.

"Together?"

"Together."

I squeal excitedly again, from both excitement and relief. My body thrums and I know deep down this is the start of something amazing between us all. I know it in my bones.

"Get off me. I'm hungry." He grumbles beneath me as Axel continues to grind both his weight and mine on top of the pile. I bark out a laugh as I try to wiggle myself free from the pile up, which earns me groans from the pair of them. I chuckle as I dash off the bed – both of them glowering at me as they lay in the pile together.

"Pizza and movie in bed?" I throw the question out there with a huge smile on my face - my muscles coil as I wait for their answer.

"Hell yes!" they both boom, jumping to their feet. I take off like a bat out of hell – running like my arse is on fire down the hallway with both of them thundering down behind me. I laugh, a lighthearted one, filled with happiness, for the first time in I don't even know how long?

I crash through my room door, laughing my arse off as I run over to the bed – with my impression of a dolphin. I dive, chuckling as I hit it with a thud and nearly bend in half as I bounce off the mattress and crash into the wall at the top near the pillows.

"Shit, Majesty. You ok?" Axel asks between labored breathes as I untangle myself from the massive pile of pillows above my head. As my eyes connect with theirs, I burst out laughing again.

"Yep. Who's ordering food?" I wiggle myself around and elbow the pillows behind me to get myself comfortable as I grab the remote at my side and hit the button. My smile widens as I watch their mouths drop open as the TV descends on the platform from the roof.

"What the?" Rafe asks in awe.

"Ha! Ms. Jeanette had it put in before I moved in. But she forgot to tell me it was here." I say as a way of an explanation.

"But you have that huge TV over there?" Axel says as he throws a thumb over his shoulder to point out the TV across from the huge sectional.

"Yeah, I know but she knows how much I like to watch TV while I'm in bed," I say with a shrug. That was a funny conversation to have with her – when I explained us Brits have a tendency to watch TV in bed. She looked at me like I was an alien and then told me Brits are weird.

"I want one in my room for when y'all piss me off," Axel chuffs as he dives across the bed – without much grace, flopping down. His weight dips the mattress so much that I'm launched into the air with a screech. Both of them are laughing as I hit the mattress with zero grace on my part.

"Food should be on its way soon," Rafe announces with a huge smile across his face. I snuggle down into the pile of pillows with a content sigh as Axel flicks through the movies on Netflix. They both roll in closer, so I'm sandwiched between the pair of them. Axel on my left and Rafe on my right – both of them arguing about which film we should watch. My eyes catch a shadow near the door, I narrow my eyes a little but relax when I see Knox and Deacon peeking through the crack in the door. I give them a soft smile as the boys continue to argue – Knox smirks then winks at me, and Deacon smiles wide as his eyes flick between the boys. *'Good Girl'* he mouths to me and I feel a thrum of excitement pass through me.

Music cuts through the room, my head whipping side to side in shock as I glare at the two guys. The two of them chuckle as my eyes land on the screen as the opening scene of my favorite film starts.

"No fucking way!" I squeal as I launch myself at Axel. He laughs harder as I kiss the side of his neck. I pull myself off and dive on Rafe next who laughs too as I kiss his neck in my excitement. "I thought you hated this?" I ask with a bemused smirk at Axel who smirks at me in that sexy way of his.

"It's your favorite. So, I'm thinking an Underworld movie marathon?" he says. I nod my head with eagerness as I spin around and wiggle until I'm comfortable. My eyes never breaking from the screen as I feel the bed move beneath me with their laughter. I watch the scenes unfold on the screen, relaxing with each passing minute. My stomach begins to rumble as I feel my muscles relax and release all the stress they've been holding for so long. My eyes grow heavier by the second. I hear Rafe grumbling at my side about the food taking too long and I smile at that.

My eyes flutter open with a soft sigh as I feel weight pressing in on me from my side. I snuggle closer not wanting to wake up, as warm air brushes across my cheeks. "Morning gorgeous," the words are spoken with a soft hum. I peel my eyes open begrudgingly as I don't want to break the spell, but I do. Rafe lays at my side snuggled into the cover with a content look on his face. I throw up a thank you for me finding this gorgeous man and having him in my life.

"Morning babe," I say with a purr. My smile widens as his eyes snap open, and a smile tips the edge of his mouth. I shuffle myself closer, so we're nose to nose. He wraps his arm around my back, trying to pull me in closer and I laugh as our foreheads connect.

"Ow!" he groans, pulling a laugh from me. I drop a kiss onto his forehead to sooth his pain and he quiets – looking at me with a lifted brow. I smile again dropping a kiss onto his lips and pulling away quickly. He growls as he pulls me back – our lips connecting again. But this time the kiss is deeper, and his chest rumbles. I try to break our kiss, but his hold on my arse tightens as his tongue licks across my bottom lip. I moan, opening up for him as he rolls me onto my back. Deepening the kiss further, my hands wrap around the back of his neck trying to pull him closer. I feel his length pressing into my thigh, and I smile as I feel how hard he is for me.

"Morning you two," Ms. Jeanette says with a jolly tone as she strolls into the room. "Now, now. You didn't eat last night, missy, and there are things to be done today," she says in a mocking stern tone. Our lips break, I smile wide at the woman who's standing at the end of the bed glaring at the back of Rafe's head. He throws daggers right back, grumbling under his breath.

"Ms. Jeanette have you see Axel this morning?" he asks to change the subject and make her forget about what we were up too.

"He does what he does boy, you know he disappears sometimes without any warning," she replies. "Don't think I didn't hear you grumbling either," her eyes narrow and she tut's at him with a warm smile on her face. I bark out a laugh, rolling away. He growls at me as he tries to pull me back in and I jump off the bed and laugh even more at the deflated look he throws my way.

"Out with you now young man," she shoos him with her hands on her hips.

I chuckle as I saunter over to the ensuite, still chuckling as I flip the shower on and strip out of my sleep shorts and top. I can still hear them bickering as I step in, the hot water like a balm to my body. I hear the cussing then the door slam, shaking my head at the temper tantrum he's just pulled knowing full well he's going to get chewed out for that later. I grab the berry shampoo, with a generous amount I lather it into my long platinum locks, while my mind works out what I need to grab today before the shit show that will happen on Monday.

The last of the suds roll off my hair, and I grab the towel off its hook and wrap it around myself. I head back into the room finding it empty and the room door ajar. I scrunch my forehead as I grab my jeans and t-shirt from the chair at the vanity and dry off quickly. I start pulling my hair up into a messy bun.

"How are you feeling?" the deep rumble of the voice has goose bumps popping up on my arm. Heat instantly pools between my legs, and I feel excitement thrum through me. I look over my shoulder as Deacon strolls into my room like some kind of avenging angel – with his black jeans and fitted black t-shirt. My eyes lazily run up and down the length of his body taking in my fill of him. The smirk spreads slowly across his face as he watches me.

"You enjoying the view?" he purrs with a deep rumble, that I feel in my centre again. I'm still in awe at his voice. Someone that looks like he did when we first met shouldn't have a voice like that. The way it affects me just from him speaking is mesmerizing but also terrifying. "You've got a little…" his thumb swipes away from the corner of my mouth and I shudder again. My eyes widen as I stare at him, the smile turns from a smirk to a huge grin - as his face turns too something a predator would have with its prey in its sights.

"I know Knox is in here tonight but tomorrow you are mine," he rumbles, I feel the vibrations through his chest as he looks down at me. I open my mouth to say something, but the words won't budge, it's as if they're stuck in the back of my throat in a thick lump. His smile turns darker, and I feel my already damp underwear become soaked. With a chaste kiss on my forehead, he strolls out of the room with long powerful strides.

I'm left standing here with my mouth hanging open. He just walked out, leaving me horny as fuck. What the actual fuck?

CHAPTER FIVE

The sales assistant behind the counter gapes at me as she sees the total on the register. I throw daggers her way. "Can you hurry up please. I have things to do?" I grumble as she takes my credit card with a trembling hand.

"Sorry, Miss Walker," she mumbles apologetically, and I have to hold back the scoff. I don't mean to be a bitch, but I can't do with any more pitying looks or the hushed whispers when I enter a store. It's really starting to pluck on my last nerve, and I feel that rattled at that moment, I think I'm about half a second away from high fiving someone in the face. She hands me back my card with a sheepish smile and passes me the fancy bags with all the essentials for the Academy. I smile as nicely as I can when she flinches back away from the counter. *Real smooth Bo, you must look like a psychopath.*

I rush out of the store, without any consideration for others as I barge through the two girls who've just come through the door. As soon as the fresh air hits my face with the breeze, I take a deep inhale and try to centre myself. That doesn't happen as the feeling of being watched passes over me, like the caress of unwelcome fingers. My head whips left and right and I really wish I hadn't. Almost everyone on the street is staring at me, some have a look of sadness on their faces – while others look like they want to tear my face off.

I stride forward, with my chin tucked into my chest. I move through the street blindly as I try to think of somewhere to go. *"You stupid cow!"* I chastise myself internally. *"You should've let one of the guys come with you like they wanted to."* Ugh, I can't be dealing with them when it comes to the outside world. One minute we're ok, then the next they're all freaking out that I'm going to have a meltdown again. It's like one second, we're in a happy content bubble, and then the next *bam!*

A bell dings as I push through a door, not having the courage to lift my head. "Good afternoon, Miss Walker would you like your usual?" My head snaps up, and my eyes connect with a bright smiled girl. I narrow my eyes a little, I look around me and relax when I realize where I am. I inhale the scent of freshly brewed coffee, and my eyes land on Justine again. She's smiling.

"Sorry for coming across rude," I say with a soft tone.

"It's ok. Has it been one of them days for you?" she asks sweetly. "Usual?" I nod my head to confirm when I notice that the noise has quieted. I look around me to find a couple of the occupants staring at me and whispering to others at their table. I bite my lip, trying to hold back the snarl.

"Get back to what you're doing!" A strong commanding voice fills the air. My head whips around to find Angie glowering at the customers as she wipes her hands on the front of her apron. I smile widely at the older woman, who looks to be ready to go to war.

"How are you, Bo?" she asks as she makes her way over to me.

"Meh," I say, and she smiles - she's an unusual sort of woman. She has the whole Bohemian vibe going on with a twist of hippie, but the commanding nature she has just oozes out of her filling the air. She's also a close friend of Ms. Jeanette. Honestly, I think the women are a great match as friends – the laughs we've shared have been some of my favorite things. They are like naughty school kids together, both are bad influences on each other.

"Ignore the sheep and relax," she says ushering me to the empty booth on the far side of the coffee house. The Lava Bean is one of my favorite places in this town, the drinks are to die for and the food that's served here is just as good as Ms. Jeanette's.

It's not long before Justine comes over with a tray balanced perfectly on her hand. My anxiety peaks a little every time I see it wobble precariously as she moves. I've always been mesmerized that the waitresses never drop a tray. She places my flat white with a shot of vanilla and a dusting of cinnamon on top. Yeah, I know it sounds gross, but I love it. It also reminds me of my mum. A blueberry muffin and a chicken and bacon sandwich are put down next – my stomach rumbles as soon as I see it. "Justine, could I grab a mint chocolate chip cooler, too, please?"

She smiles at me, nodding her head. It's been a long time since I've ordered one of them, but I want it for my way back home. The first bite of my sandwich has me groaning as the flavor has a field day on my taste buds. I start to relax as the food and coffee take me down memory lane, thankfully the customers have gone back to what they're doing.

"He's probably happy he's dead. Now he doesn't have to see your whoreish face anymore," a voice snarls from somewhere behind me. My limbs lock up at the words, as Jade steps into view with a savage smile on her face. The room instantly quiets as she glares daggers at me.

"Look at you sitting here like the Queen, while we all know

you're a murderer, bitch." she growls with a hand on her hip. "What's the matter trailer trash? Cat got your tongue?" My brain explodes as my hands start to tremble - I pull myself to my feet with a savage snarl of my own.

"You fucking what now?" I demand with a harsh tone; her eyes widen a touch, but a smirk tips the edge of her lips as I step out of the booth.

"You fucking heard me whore," she screeches with a high-pitched nasally tone. I growl then, in warning, but she doesn't back down. She steps closer to me in challenge, and my smile turns predatory as I snarl at her again. "You are nothing but a disease." She booms, my hand runs across the edge of the table as I try to keep my calm.

"Jade!" Angie barks. "Get out of here now," she demands. Jade scoffs at this, taking her attention off me and turning it towards Angie.

"Now why would I want to do that?" She says with a sarcastic lilt to her tone. "Everyone in the town knows she's a disease. Frost died because of her," she spits. My rage roars through me as my whole body begins to shake violently, I can feel the tears from my anger begin to pool in my eyes. She turns her attention back to me; her smile is all teeth as she looks me up and down. "First her parents and then Frost."

Angie shouts something, as my vision tunnels towards its sole focus. The bitch that's standing in front of me, the look of triumph on her face, as a tear escapes the corner of my eye - carving a path down my cheek. Murmurs break out around the room. "Bo. Calm down," someone shouts from within the room, but their voice doesn't sound like anyone I know. But that's the thing, when your rage takes over everything starts to disappear until you're focused on one thing.

I protected her when I didn't have to. I put a bigger target on my back for her. Then, she turns into this. I thought the obsession with that arsehole was bad enough. But to stand here like she's the new Wankstein and push me when she knows what I'm capable of? It's either brave or stupid!

"Yeah, as I've told you before, she's a disease. Look at what happened to Frost and Cassandra just months after she got here," she says to someone. I step closer, bringing us chest to chest. Her head whips around to face me as she lifts her chin and looks down her nose at me as all the elitists do. "We. Don't. Want. You. In. Our. Tow…"

I lash out, the urge to cause pain turning me into a savage being, a blood curdling scream fills the air. As she frantically swipes at her eyes, I smile savagely as the empty cup crashes to the ground like a deafening tune, people scream as Jade stumbles around trying to clear the drink out of her eyes. I inch even closer about to finish what I started when someone pulls her out of my way – the sound that escapes me is horrifying. The woman instantly pales.

"Bo?" someone says but I can only just make it out as my attention is riveted, watching her rock back and forth as the woman tries to console her – it doesn't bring me the satisfaction I thought it would.

"Bo?" I spin on my heels grabbing my stuff and my eyes connect with Angie's – seeing hers filled with horror and concern has the emotions roaring to life even harder. My chest rises and falls rapidly – but I don't say anything as I stride out of the building, slamming the door behind me. Sirens wail in the distance as I stand on the sidewalk, the weight of emotions crushing my chest. My hands shake as I try to regulate my breathing but the breaths get harsher with each minute. The heaviness in my chest continues to grow, everything is too much. I throw my head back and scream, the sound ear splitting as I pour everything into it – anger and pain at this shitshow that is now my life.

The sound fills the air with a horrid, broken, and hollow kind of sound. I push all the emotions over the last few weeks into it – trying to expel the feelings from my body with that scream. The scream dies down, breaking off into a broken sob as my chin lands on my chest. A numbness fills me again, keeping my feet planted to my spot. My head snaps up as the feeling of being watched crashes over me, and I connect with the bluest eyes, that I now only ever see in my nightmares. Frost stands on the opposite side of the street, staring at me with the corner of his mouth tipped up in his usual smirk. "Why're you doing this to me?" I scream at him, my bottom lip trembles as I feel the pressure building more intensely at the back of my eyes. The tears start to spill over as I watch the smirk change into a savage smile. I step off the curb, keeping my eyes on him. The urge to demand answers is my driving force – a horn blares as my head snaps right, seeing the car hurtling towards me. I'm frozen just staring at it, as the driver hits the brakes and they screech in protest – but, still, it keeps on coming.

"What the fuck do you think you're doing?" a panicked voice bellows. Pain roars through my back as my lids flutter open but all I see is the blue sky. Knox's panicked face blocks out the view as he peers down at me with wide eyes. "What're you trying to do?" he booms, "Why the fuck are you trying to kill yourself?" he demands his face taut.

"Oh my god, I'm so sorry," someone says, Knox pulls his attention away from me. "Thank god you pulled her out of the way."

"Get the fuck out of here now," he roars, I hear a squeak then a car screeches – he turns his attention back to me, the whites of his eyes showing.

I tentatively lift my hand to his face, smiling weakly as the stubble on his face scratches against my palm. His eyes close as he pushes his cheek into my hand – his eyes snap open to stare at me. He blows out a harsh breath, his hand tickling the side of my neck as it moves around, and he firmly grips the back of my hair at the nape of my neck. He yanks me up onto my feet, bringing us nose to nose. His brows furrow as he looks between my eyes – trying to see if he can work out what's going on in my mind.

"Do you know what would happen to us if anything happened to you?" his rough voice croaks. I stare at him dumfounded; I don't even try to say anything. "If you go, we all go." He declares with a growl. "I don't want to be in a world where you aren't. So, answer me. What in the hell do you think you were doing?"

"I saw him," I rush through my words. "He's right…." My words break off as I find the spot where Frost was now empty.

"Babe," the words are pushed out through his teeth as his eyes narrow just a little. His face smooths out just as quickly, but it was there. The look of pity. "You can't keep doing this. We're worried about you, and I think it's a good idea if you speak to someone about your hallucinations."

"I'm not crazy!" I demand, pushing against his chest. He reluctantly pulls back giving me some much needed space. I glower at him. His eyes meet mine as he stands to his full height forcing me to crane my neck to be able to see him. "I. Am. Not. Going. Crazy," I snap as I spin on my heel, the click of phones catches my attention as people stand on either side of the road snapping photos of my outburst. I growl, striding down the pavement to get away from him, and the people that I know are going to add my life to social media, once again. I don't bother with the bags I had, either. The need to get away as quickly as I can is the only thing that matters, at the moment. He bellows after me, but I don't stop or turn around even though he's begging me to listen to him.

I've heard the guys whispering when they think I'm not paying attention about how they want me to talk to someone, but I know I'm not crazy. The pounding of my boots against the pavement helps relieve some of the emotions – making it easier for me to think things through. But then the weird thoughts start and I'm beginning to wonder if the guys are right?

CHAPTER SIX

M y body screams in agony as I unfurl myself from the park bench, my eyes watering as they sting at being assaulted by the sunshine and the fact that I haven't slept a wink all night. I just laid my ass down on the wooden bench with my hoodie underneath me as a pillow. Thank God it wasn't too cold last night, meaning I didn't have to give up my protest and head home. My phone died sometime through the night, so I don't have a clue what time it is.

"Are you planning on avoiding us forever?" the deep tenor of the voice has my toes curling. I smile despite feeling guilty that I've caused them all stress. It's as clear as day with the lines creasing the edges of his eyes. Deacon doesn't smile at me as I shuffle myself down the bench so we're closer.

"They're worried about you, c'mon," he says with an outstretched hand. I take it and he pulls me too my feet. We head out towards the statue in the centre of the park, and I see his car parked haphazardly against the pavement. I look to him to try and see what is going on inside his head, and he turns his head to stare at me. I smile sweetly to try and reassure him I am fine, but his returning smile is strained.

Neither of us say a word as we climb into the car and before I know it, we're pulling out into traffic and making our way home.

The drive back was quiet, which is a little unsettling as I expected him to chew me out on the drive over. But he didn't. The front door looms in front of me as I climb out, apprehension filling me. I walk through the door, feeling like I'm about to step in front of a firing squad when I realize there's an eerie sort of quiet in the house. There is none of the laughter or shouting that normally echoes off the walls with a house full of guys.

"I'm so happy he found you child," Ms. Jeanette coos, rushing over to me from the kitchen. "Don't ever do that to us again," she snaps, and my head droops as the weight of what I put them through hits me.

"Do they know we're here?" he asks with a heavy brooding tone, my toes curl again and heat spreads across my skin like wildfire. I feel like I'm watching a tennis match as my head ping pongs between the pair of them.

"Everyone is out at the moment," she says as she turns her attention back to me. With a soft smile and gentle squeeze of my forearm she heads back towards the kitchen. A tug on my hand has me looking to Deacon, who nods his head towards the stairs. I follow him up as we make our way up and he keeps the pressure on my hand.

I'm surprised when he pushes through his room door, dragging me behind him as I stumble through the door with the force. He spins around and closes the door with a definitive click, my heart stutters a little at the sound of the lock.

"Do you understand how worried I was about you?" The deep baritone of his voice rumbles, and I can hear the rattle of his chest.

"I'm sorry," I croak, my throat closing making it feel like it's trying to suffocate me.

"You're sorry what?" He demands with a quirked brow, as he folds his arms across his chest. I feel my core heat with anticipation, but my mouth dries almost instantly.

"I'm sorry, Rocket." I rush out. "I just needed some time to process everything. Jade pissed me off. Then, Knox looks at me like you all have been for last few weeks and it was too much." My chest rises and falls rapidly as I drop my chin, breaking eye contact with him. I feel the moisture prick at my eyes again – I should've come home. I gasp as a hard grasp holds my chin, tilting it up so I am eye to eye with him, and I see all the emotions he's feeling flicking across his eyes.

"On your knees," he commands, and I drop to the floor without any quick comeback. I can feel it in the tremble of his hand, that this is something he needs.

I stare at his feet, not daring to look up for the first time. "Good girl," I hear the smile in his voice, and I have to fight one of my own. I think he thought I was going to fight him on this. "I'm too wound up for anything less than brutal at the moment, but I have to have you."

My core clenches at this as I feel my underwear get soaked, "Take me out and show me how sorry you are for having me worry."

I nod my head without lifting it, he growls, and I can hear the vibration in his chest. I grasp his jeans, pulling him closer to me as I rise onto my knees. Undoing his button, the sound of the zipper coming down, and one quick plop are the only things to be heard apart from our breathing. I pull his jeans down, and his length springs free from the confinement – my mouth waters as I spot the bead of pre-come on his tip. I yank his jeans down as far as they will go as I wrap my lips around his tip swirling my tongue around – groaning as the taste of the bead hits my tongue. I can't resist the urge any longer and swallow him down as far back as I can get him, pulling a groan from him. I gag as he hits the back of my throat – breathing the best I can through my nose. I try to push him past my reflex, but a hand stops me as I feel my hair prickling on my scalp as the tension builds and he pulls out of my mouth.

"Keep your mouth like this and hold on," he snarls as he slams into my mouth, hitting the back of my throat and I have to fight with everything in me not to gag.

Back and forth he pulls out and pushes in, trying to get his cock past my gag reflex. His hold on me is brutal as he fucks my mouth with a ferocity I've never seen in him before. Tears stream down my face as he continues to fuck my mouth like a man possessed. My clit is throbbing between my legs begging for the release I'm so desperately craving as I listen to the moans he's making. I keep one hand on his thigh to leverage myself as I plunge my hand into my leggings, trying to push past the gathered fabric to the aching nub.

"Do not touch yourself," he demands as his thrusts become frantic. I fight to breathe but the need to relieve some of the torment is too much. I cry out as he rips himself free of my mouth and his hand tightens to the point of agonizing pain, I whimper as my head is pulled back and his eyes settle on mine. There's a darkness in him that I haven't seen since the day of the incident, and I fight to hold back my moan.

He pulls me off my knees with the hold he has on me, forcing me to hiss at the pain as my eyes water. His snarl is savage as he slams me against the wall at the side of the door. I can't get air into my lungs as his weight presses into me – he nips at my lobe causing a shudder to pass through me.

"Do you understand how frantic you have us all at any given time of the day?" he rumbles into my ear, his breathe tickling the shell. I whimper again and I can hear the smile with the growl he rumbles. "Do you see how feral you make me?"

"Yes, Rocket," I breathe out between my teeth as I fight the moan trying to break free.

His grin is predatory as he looks into my eyes, everything is hidden from me and I daren't voice the fear that's creeping its way up my spine. I know he would never intentionally hurt me, but this is a side of Deacon I only ever catch glimpses off.

"Are you going to be a good girl and hold on?" he purrs into my ear causing me to shudder. The tearing of fabric has me gasping as cold air hits my core, I look down to see him pulling away the material of my leggings to reveal the hole he's just made.

"Don't make a sound," he commands. My head snaps up to connect with his gaze as I open my mouth to ask him what he means. I scream as he slams into me, the feel of him stretching me is too much as I pant. His hand comes up to cover my mouth, stopping me from talking as he pulls out and slams into me again. I gasp every time he fills me, but then my core clenches to try and keep him in place as he withdraws. I whimper at the loss of connection every time but then his eyes narrow and I have to bite my lip behind his hand to keep myself quiet.

The sensation builds I can feel the start of a mind-blowing orgasm begin to build, then he withdraws. His chest heaving as he stares intently into my eyes – as soon as the tingles disappear, he starts his movements again. Bringing me to the brink each time and just when I'm about to fall over the edge, he stops. My body trembles, the desperation to be able to come is becoming too much. His moans are becoming louder – his thrusts more painful and desperate.

"Rocket, please," I beg, my lower lip trembling at the vortex of emotions building inside me. His head snaps up to meet my gaze, that's when I notice his hand isn't covering my mouth, so my words were clear.

"I told you to stay quiet," he booms, not slowing his pace at all. My nails dig into his shoulders as I hold on, while also trying to coax him into giving me what I need.

I feel him swell, I grind down on him to try and bring myself to the ledge. He snarls forcing my shoulders back against the wall, stopping my movements. His roar is loud as I feel him explode – his chest rising and falling rapidly as he drops his head to his chest in ecstasy. My legs tremble, sweat runs down between my shoulder blades, my chest rising and falling as the emotions become as strong as a hurricane. I wince as he pulls out, I pant as I clench my fists. He releases his hold on me and my body is that weak, I crash to the floor in a heap. Tears begin to pool in my eyes – he denied me. Why? Because he's mad that I disappeared to clear my head? Or because he says he was worried?

My teeth grind as all the emotions hit me like a Mac truck. I pull myself up onto shaking legs trying to keep myself upright as I narrow my eyes on him. As if he can feel me, he lifts his head to meet mine.

"Now you know how you make us feel," he says with a softer tone this time. I bite harder into my lip not saying a word as he takes a step towards me. There isn't the harshness in his eyes like earlier; the man before me is the person I know. The crack resonates around the room. Deacon stumbles back with wide eyes, as my palm starts to sting from the impact across his face. Tears fight to break free, but I manage to hold them at bay.

"You deny me because you're pissed that I wandered off?" I spit between clenched teeth. The emotions have taken on a life of their own now and I'm just a passenger. "What was this? Some sick and twisted revenge because you got scared?"

"We were all terrified something had happened to you," he shouts back, pulling himself up to his full height. I can see the red print begin to take shape on his face. "I love you!"

"That's not love," I spit back taking a step closer. "You did to me exactly what he did that day at the theme park." I see his eyes widen and then the guilt is as clear as day on his face as his adam's apple bobs with a gulp.

"You used me to get out your emotions, to get back at me because you're pissed I didn't do what you wanted," I snarl as I sidestep around him, bringing my back closer to the door. "He spat his dummy out too because he didn't get his way. But you? I never thought you would do this to me." The last word comes out broken as I fight to keep the tears back. He steps towards me, and I step back. My hand bumps the door handle, so I twist stepping out into the hallway.

"Bo?"

"Stay the fuck away from me," I snarl spinning on my heel and striding down the hallway to my room. His feet pound the floor behind me, I pick up my pace until my heart pounds as my strides eat up the ground to stay in front of him. I throw my door open just as he catches up to me, I slam the door in his face – clicking the lock into place. I turn the other two that I recently had installed to give me the privacy I sometimes crave. He bellows my name from the other side, as his fists pound on the door. I grab my headphones from the coffee table, slipping them on I crank up the music.

CHAPTER SEVEN

I stare at my reflection in the mirror, and a weird sort of numbness settles over me. I thought I would be a ball of anxiety going back to the academy today. I know shit's about to go down there, as I take my place where I'm meant to be, but I really don't give a shit about it. It's time to go and face the hyenas. With a deep breath, I twist and turn making sure everything is in its place. I grab my bag from beside my nightstand. I take slow breaths in and out as I step out into the hallway. Voices fill the air as someone bangs around in the kitchen.

"You look fit to rule," a soft voice has me looking to my right. Ms. Jeanette stands there with a wide smile on her face, which has my muscles relaxing a touch. "I don't know what went on the other night," she begins to say. I grind my teeth together as the emotions roar to the surface once more. At my reaction she closes her eyes and inhales deeply. "Are you ready for what's about to come?" she asks with a small voice. I can see the worry lining her face. My heart thaws a little as I pull her into me for a hug. She comes willingly and I smile as I hug the woman who is the constant in my life since being here.

"The student body will do what they do best – but I'm ready to bring them in line, if need be," I say with a determined tone. This is my town, my academy, and no jumped-up rich bastards are going to disturb this.

The smile that stretches across her face is full of pride as I turn on my heel and head down the hallway. Once at the top of the stairs I can hear the guys laughing and joking with each other. My heart spasms a little in my chest as I paste a huge smile on my face. I descend the stairs with Ms. Jeanette at my back, with my combat boots making a thud on each step, and the noise in the kitchen stops. Stools scrape as Rafe comes into view first, and his eyes widen as he takes me in. Then, a smirk spreads across his face. Knox comes in next, and he nods his head to me in greeting then diverts his eyes. Looks like he's just as salty as he was the other day.

Deacon comes in next. His hair is sticking out all over the place and there are thick dark circles under his eyes. His uniform is creased and sticking out all over the place. He is the exact opposite of his normal put together look. He takes a step towards me but stops when Ms. Jeanette clears her throat. I look over my shoulder at her and she smiles encouragingly – this right here is why I love her. Axel comes in and my eyes nearly roll out of my head across the floor, Rafe bursts out laughing as I look between all four of them.

"You didn't think I was going to let you face the hyenas with just these three did you Majesty?" I fight to hold back the smirk that's trying to tip the edge of my mouth. I should have known he was up to something when Ms. Jeanette told me he had gone to see Mr. Geoffrey.

"I know we're having issues, but today we need to show a united front to the other students because you know as well as I do, if they smell blood they will strike." I say, looking between them. They all nod their heads in acknowledgement. "I know we have things to discuss but today is not the day. Now, let's get this over with," I command as I head out of the front door towards my Camaro. I climb in, a ball of mixed emotions heavy in my stomach, and my head snaps to the side as the passenger door opens. I'm just about to yell at Rafe when Axel drops into the seat with a huge grin on his face.

"They sent you to babysit?" I accuse with a glare; his eyes narrow a little as he growls in the back of his throat.

"No, I wanted to check and see if you're ok after the other night?"

"You mean when Deacon decided to channel his inner Frost?" I snarl, the feeling has me wanting to toss his ass out of the car so I can be on my own.

"I know what he did was wrong but..."

"Don't you fucking dare defend him!" I spit, throwing the car into gear and peeling out of the drive with a screech of tires. "Don't sit there and tell me he didn't mean it," I snap.

My hand white knuckles the wheel, as we shoot up the drive towards the gates. I don't slow down as we get closer, and Axel starts to fidget beside me which brings a sadistic smile to my lips.

"Bo?" He sounds panicked as the metal gets closer.

I chuckle, the sound harsh and short as I turn my head to keep my eyes on him as my foot presses harder on the accelerator.

"Don't play, Majesty. This isn't funny," he shouts, and the terror is clear in his voice.

"It kinda is," I laugh, as Knox frantically beeps his horn behind us. I can see the gate getting closer, I smile savagely as his yells become more horrified. I slam my foot down and whoop as the brakes squeal for all they're worth, and the back end of the car slides as we come to a screeching halt, right in front of the gates. I chuckle as the realization dawns on me, if

I'd have waited just a second longer, we would've been eating metal.

"Look I'm sorry for the asshole Deacon, but please don't kill me just because you're mad at him," he says between pants. I quirk a brow at him, my own chest rising and falling rapidly as I try not to think of how stupid I'm being. "I know you're pissed with Knox, too. But Majesty, I'm too pretty to die."

He smacks his forehead and I chuckle again. Doors slamming closed catch my attention and I see the others running to the car – Knox bangs on my window and I growl as I hit the button.

"What the fuck are you playing at?" he snarls, through the crack of the window, death glaring me.

"Watch your tone asshat," I retort with a snarl of my own. "I got bored and decided to scare the shit out of Axel." I shrug, turning my attention away from him.

"We're going to be late," I say after another minute – he mumbles something under his breath as he makes his way back to the car. Rafe's and Deacon's heads ping pong between my car and theirs but thankfully they don't approach. I blow out a harsh breath that sounds more of a whistle between my teeth as Knox reverses giving me enough space to move my car back to allow the gates to open. A message pops on my screen from Ms. Jeanette, telling me not to murder anyone today because she won't bail me out. I laugh, screeching out of the driveaway onto the road, and head off to the hell hole.

The car park is almost full as I tear ass into the first spot I find empty. *"Welcome to the start of a new term Bo,"* I snark to myself. Everyone's heads snap around to face the car, and eyes widen as others' narrow on me. I take a deep breath, knuckles still white on the wheel finding it hard to let go.

"We've got you," Axel purrs at my side – giving my thigh a squeeze in support. The contact breaks me out of my spell and I grab my bag from the back of the car throwing my door open just as Knox peels into the spot next to mine. I climb out, the whispers hitting my ears instantly. I can't make out what's being said but it sets my nerves on fire, regardless.

I round the front of the car waiting for the others to join me as I throw the odd occasional dagger at the ones who are whispering the loudest.

"Why would she even come back here?" is the one I hear the most or *"How can she stand there like she's not to blame for killing him?"*

I try to count to ten in my head, so I don't beat the fuckers' faces in, but it's proving difficult. A hand wraps around my waist pulling me closer, and my head whips up to find Axel looking down at me with a soft smile. "You've got this," he whispers, and I smile a little at his encouragement. Honestly, I'm glad he's here with how strained it is between me and the other two. He and Rafe have been the support network I never knew I really needed until recently.

"What the fuck are you looking at?" Knox's voice booms across the campus grounds causing all the people present to divert their eyes. The screech of static fills the air causing all of us to wince.

"Students are to report to the Auditorium before classes commence for a special assembly."

Dread fills me as my legs feel like dead weights. With Axel's support, I manage to put one foot in front of the other, but it feels like I'm walking through sludge. We follow the student body who are making their way to the building which houses the auditorium, some of them throwing looks over their shoulders as they pass through the doors. I quickly pull away from Axel and stand up straighter even though I feel like I'm going to collapse, I can't show them any weakness. So, with my best resting bitch face on I stride into the room, pushing some people out of the way.

I spot some seats in the back row empty, and I dash forward claiming them as ours as I take a seat and glare at anyone who tries to sit on my left side. They scurry off, moving to find empty ones lower down, when I notice the huge projector behind the dean.

"What the fuck is going on?" I hiss, all the guys look at me with suspicion lining their faces.

"Thank you for joining us after the break, it's with a sad heart we are doing this today." The dean says with a sad tone, my brows hit my hairline. How can the dean say that with a straight face, because Frost made life hell for the faculty here. All the other faculty members are sitting in a row behind the dean with sad expressions on their faces. They're all full of shit, and we all know every single one of them hated him.

Mournful music blares through the speakers pulling my attention back into the present – as the projector lights up and my heart drops into my feet. "We lost an amazing student recently, and that will forever sit heavy in our hearts. So please pay attention to the memorial video we have put together for Kenton Frost."

His eyes stare at me as his academy picture flashes up on the screen, my heart stutters as my eyes take in Frost in his uniform. I watch as one picture moves to another, then another as the music continues to pull at my nerves making me shuffle uncomfortably in my seat.

"Breathe, its ok," a voice coos at the side of me trying to soothe me but it just makes me grind my teeth as voices fill the air. I narrow my gaze as videos start to pop up from other students saying how much of an amazing guy he was and how he will be missed. It would hurt less if they ripped my heart out of my chest while I was awake and stab it repeatedly with a sharp object.

Sobbing fills the air, and my attention is pulled to the video at the bottom corner of the screen. Wankstein stands there with tears streaming down her face, saying she's devastated that's she's lost the love of her life. Pain roars to life in my fingertips as I squeeze my seat with everything I have, and I can feel my nails protesting against the solid bottom. My teeth grind as my gaze zeros in on the bitch four rows down in front of me. I close my eyes, counting to ten, to try and stop the urge to climb over the chairs and rip her head off.

Finally, the music begins to subside, and chatter fills the air. The dean barks into the microphone quieting everyone. A few don't listen, and the noise begins to pick up in volume again.

"Quiet!" the dean barks, making the microphone screech through the speakers. I wince as the noise assaults my ears, "We have another announcement. We have a new student joining us at the academy please will you welcome…"

White noise fills my ears as my mouth drops open. *What the actual fuck?* I can't do anything but stare. Voices surround me, some louder than others as I try to process what I can see in front of me. People jump to their feet as my mind races. I jump to my feet, my head swinging left to right as I search for the person in the chaos. I spot the mucky blonde hair as he leaves through the doors. I jump over the back of my seat rushing through the door – breathing labored. I spin in a slow circle.

"You looking for me?" I shiver as the tone caresses my skin making goosebumps pebble along my flesh.

"How are you here?" I demand in a broken tone, my mind still reeling. Anger roars to life as he strides away from me across the grass. I chase after him, the need for answers fueling me.

"Don't you fucking dare walk away from me!" I scream, as I chase after the person who has been haunting me. "We buried you."

My whole body trembles violently as I continue my pursuit. How has the last few weeks of my life been a lie? Why have I grieved and haunted myself with guilt and he wasn't even dead?

"Frost! Stop, dammit."

I have to skid to a stop to avoid crashing into him, when he rounds on me. His face full of fury, as he looks me up and down. Tears escape the corners of my eyes at the relief of him being here, with us, with me. His hand snaps out, I gasp as my throat is restricted stopping air form reaching my lungs. His eyes narrow even further as he snarls stepping into me, the hand tightening around my throat with enough force to cause my knees to buckle.

"My name is Kylo Brookes," he snarls, stray spit hitting my cheek as he presses closer. "You killed my fucking brother!"

The tears stream down my face now as everything swirls within in me, I start to feel light-headed as my brain becomes fuzzy and the pressure on my neck becomes even heavier. "I don't understand," the words come out choppy as I try to get enough air into my lungs that are now screaming. "Frost was my brother, you killed him. Now I'm here to return the favor."

I see the darkness edging closer as my vision blurs, shouts sound muffled around me and then suddenly the pressure is gone. I start coughing and gulping down air on my side as my vision straightens itself out and then becomes blurry again. "I've got you," I scramble backwards away from the voice, when I stop myself as my vision clears again and I see Axel with a pained expression on his face.

"No one puts her on her knees but me," the words boom in the air with a menacing snarl. Then, the thud of something kills the air, followed closely by cussing. Axel yanks me to my feet, and I stare horrified as Deacon savagely punches the guy who is swinging wildly too.

"Rip the bastard's head off," Knox yells egging him on.

Nausea swirls in my stomach as they continue to throw punch after punch. Deacon is holding his own with more ferocity than I knew he was capable of when chants of "fight" fill the air as the other students press in closer to the chaos.

"You may have the face of someone we knew. But you will never touch what is ours like that again," he roars landing a kick to Kylo's ribs which launches him off his feet. He hits the floor with a thud, and Deacon doesn't give him a chance as he lands blow after blow with a roar.

"Break it up," someone shouts form behind the bodies. Knox and Axel share a look, but before I have time to work out what it means, I'm being hauled across the campus. Axel keeping a tight hold of me as Knox and Rafe pull off a possessed Deacon, dragging him in the direction of the cars. Axel pushes me into the passenger seat. Slamming the door, he runs around to the other side jumping in. The engine roars to life – the tires screeching as he reverses out of the spot, I'm thrown forward from the way he slams on the brakes. I have to lift my hands to stop myself from hitting the dash. Then the tires screech once again as he wheelspins out of the carpark and back onto the main road. I look through the back window, and relief fills me as I spot Knox's car following closely behind us.

CHAPTER EIGHT

KNOX

I 'm such a fucking asshole! I was adamant that she was going nuts and I pressed the guys to seek help for her in any form we could. I even contemplated having her admitted for a little while to see if it helped. But now knowing that she wasn't going crazy at all, and she really was seeing him, well I don't blame her for that. How the fuck does he look so identical to Frost anyway?

The music thumps through the speakers with enough force to have everything vibrating from the bass. I never wanted to see that bastard again, and I've managed to avoid him since the shitshow, and he hasn't once bothered me too much. But now that I'm going willingly – I hope he will give me the answers we need. My palms become slick the closer I get to the gated community, I never noticed how peaceful it was not being housed here. Bo's house is closer to the Academy than ours, but that's not the other thing I'm happy about not seeing, his house stands empty at the top of the hill. His mom left the day after the funeral and hasn't been seen since.

The guard's box comes into view as I crawl down the street,

gearing myself to go to war with him if I need too. "Nice to see you again Aiden," James says with a nod of this head.

"You know not to call me that old man," I smirk as his eyes narrow on me.

"Sorry Knox," he retorts with a sarcastic drawl and roll of his eyes. I chuckle at the balls on the guy because the others practically piss their pants when they see one of us pull up, but not him.

"I never understood why only two of you wanted to be called your last names?" he muses, rubbing his chin. I take it as a rhetorical question and don't bother to answer – it's easier than explaining the real reason. The fact of the matter is I hate my name, always have – my grandfather was named Aiden and he was a vile man, always cruel and never once having a smile on his face for anything. But when I was born, he demanded I be named after him to carry on the Knox name and become just like him.

A horn pulls me out of my thoughts, I look into my centre mirror glaring at the Bentley behind me. Even though it's wasted effort because they can't see me, rolling the sleeve up of my shirt so my tattoos show – I put my arm out of the window and flip the fucker the bird. Surprise, surprise – the horn stops instantly. Even James chuckles at how abruptly it stops, and with a wave of his hand, he tells me to get going. The drive is a short one since I drove like a bat outta hell to pull up outside my nightmare.

My door slamming has the gardener scuttling away like a cockroach, and I burst through the door not bothering to be quiet. As I stride through the house, I notice there aren't as many of the staff as there should be. "Where is he?" I demand one of the maids, who turns white at my face. I can see the late stages of bruising on her cheek, my teeth grind together as it dawns on me. She is probably one of the ones that he fucks when he gets bored, but then gets handsy with when they don't do what he wants. She points down the hall, I nod my head in a silent thanks and take off in that direction. Raised voices catch my attention the closer I get to his office.

"What do you fucking take me for, there is nothing that can be done?"

"That's not acceptable, I want what I'm owed." Something smashes against a wall, no doubt his phone. I only caught his side of the conversation, but it doesn't take a rocket scientist to work out he's up to his usual tricks.

"I know you're there, boy," the tone has me grinding my teeth as I smooth out my face – so I give nothing away. I step through the door, taking my first look at him in weeks – he looks old. Nothing like the person who had me cowering in a corner when I was smaller.

"Who the fuck is Kylo Brookes?" I don't bother with formalities. His eyes widen a touch before his face smooths out again. Anyone else would have missed the slight dip in his features, but not me.

"I don't know who you're talking about," he says with a shrug as he pulls some papers out of a file on top of his desk. He doesn't look at me again as he reads.

"Let's try this again, shall we, asshole," I snarl stepping closer to his desk. His head snaps up as his gaze takes me in. His brow lifts as he drops the papers, leaning back in his chair. Anger flutters across his face, and I smirk as I stare back in challenge.

"You really must think the tourist is worth the beating you know you'll get from this insubordination. We both know, boy, that it won't be long before she disappears. The Walkers make a habit of that."

My hands snap out swiftly, and his eyes widen as I haul his ass over the top of the desk, slamming his back into the floor.

His eyes nearly bug out of his head, as he gets a real good look at the man I am now. I push all my weight into my knee on his chest – keeping him there.

"Watch what you say about my girl," I rumble, pressing a little more weight on him. "Tell me who the fuck Kylo Brookes is and why the fuck he is identical to Frost!" my voice booms through the room.

"You're going to regret this boy. I'm going to make your life hell for this." He snarls savagely trying to push me off of him. I laugh darkly as I wrap a hand around his throat pulling him off the floor.

"You can try, but nothing can hurt me anymore. Not even you," I declare with the weight lifting off my shoulders. Here and now, I am not worried about what he thinks he can do to me because I know he won't stand a chance because the fear I had is no longer there.

"We'll see about that," he snaps. My fist connects with his jaw, and as he falls to the ground, I react. My fists begin pounding against his flesh with the urge to show him who the scariest one of us is riding me hard. He yells for me to stop as blood flows in small rivulets down his face and the shadows peppering his face tell me he's going to be one big bruise tomorrow and that gives me a feeling of satisfaction.

"Who is he?" I demand once more. I take a step back giving him a little space to pull himself into a seated position on the office floor. He takes a cloth from the inside pocket of his suit jacket, wiping at the blood on his face. His eyes widen again when he sees how much of it there is.

"He's his twin. That should be obvious," he says. I step closer to deck him again. He holds a hand up to halt me and I see the heavy set of his shoulders deflate – as he blows out a harsh breath.

"When he found out she was expecting he was excited

about having a son to carry on his legacy and rule the town in his image. But then it changed when she told him it was twins. He became angry, then quiet, and he started having meetings with random people outside of the society." My brows drop as I frown.

"He'd decided if one was a girl, he wanted to have a suitable marriage proposition for her when she came of age and that's what the meetings were about. He was pimping out one of them before they were even born." My stomach rolls as nausea swirls, I always knew he was a cruel son of a bitch, but this is beyond anything I thought he would resort to. The image of Bo tied to the gurney has my heart stuttering as I remember what he was going to do to her to keep himself on the throne.

"But then they found out the twins were boys and he lost it over that, calling her a waste of space and demanding she rectify this. Nothing was said after that, and I thought he'd gotten over it but then the labor came, and Kenton was born first." I listen intently, my nerves feel like a live wire.

"As soon as Kylo was born, he passed him off to one of his most trusted guards and he dropped off the face of the earth. His words to me were, 'I only need one son, but it helps having the option of a spare.'"

My brain races to try and put the pieces together but no matter how I try to fit them, it seems like I haven't got all the pieces. My brows shoot up and my mouth drops open as they start to click into place. He's an evil vindictive man.

"Has anyone heard of him since he disappeared?" I demand of him, his head whips side to side with the answer no. His eyes flick between mine, and I snarl savagely as he cowers on the floor. That must be it! He dropped off the face of the earth and he knew of Kylo so it makes sense he would get him to get his revenge on her.

"He'll be coming for her son. You need to get as far away

from her as possible," he says, rising to his feet. "She's going to end this town."

"He can come for her all he wants," I admit turning to face him. "But that doesn't mean he will get anywhere near her if we've got anything to do with it."

"Don't be stupid boy. Leave and stay safe, that's what your mother would've wanted." My hands tremble as the emotions I pushed into a box a long time ago rattle in my mind. I have to fight myself so I don't kill him for mentioning her. I close my eyes taking a deep breath to center myself. Once I feel a little calmer, I open my eyes to look at him. I smile like a maniac.

"Leave this town," I demand as I turn my back to him. "I never want to see your face around here again. If you don't, make no mistakes, dad, I will end you," I say with a finality that has me feeling lighter. I make my way out of the room. He shouts my name to stop me, but I ignore his feeble attempts. I need to speak to the others, and we need a game plan.

CHAPTER NINE

BO

I can't believe he's here. Well, not him, but someone that looks just like him. *"You killed my brother. I'm here to return the favor."* The words swirl around my head on repeat, a headache starts to throb behind my eyes. I don't understand, nothing is making sense.

"He's meant to be Kylo Frost." My head whips around, eyes widening as Knox comes into the room with determined strides. His chest moving rapidly, I look behind him seeing the front door open and his car parked haphazardly against the steps.

"What're you talking about," Axel demands, jumping to his feet. A shiver passes over me as I see his face in my mind and the pure hatred that shined back at me with malice.

"They're brothers. Kylo was passed off to someone seconds after being born." He says with a haunted expression. The urge to soothe him is strong but I'm frozen in my seat not able to move.

"He's here to kill me," I croak as my throat feels like he's cutting my airway off again. All of them rush to me to offer forms of comfort, but if they're honest with themselves – they'll know it's true.

"I think this has something to do with the piece of shit that we can't find." Knox says louder to catch our attention, all of us look to him and the fierce set of his face has me feeling a small amount of happiness that I'm not the one that will be at the end of his wrath.

"He was the one who sent Kylo away and don't you think it's weird he turns up now wanting revenge when we've never heard of him?" he moves over to me, I can see the worry in his eyes. The emotions have me all over the place, I grab his wrist and pull him closer – burying my head in his chest. I breathe a sigh of relief as he encases me in his arms pulling me as close as I can get. I inhale the scent of the body wash he uses, and my muscles begin to relax a little.

"So, what do we do?" I ask in a small voice, as I pull free of his grip and look around at them all.

"We need to play it cool and try and figure out why he's here," Axel says as he moves away from the island as he pulls out his phone and fires off a message to someone. "I've just messaged my uncle. If anyone can find out where he's come from, it's him," Axel says with a warm smile in my direction.

"It's going to be chaos tomorrow. We left after Deacon lost his shit and got into a brawl with him and if he's anything like his brother, you all know as well as I do, he will have used our absence to his benefit." I say as I slide out of my seat, and my muscles protest as an overwhelming feeling of tiredness hits me.

"Agreed."

I smile softly to them as I head out of them room and up the stairs. With each step my legs become heavier until I'm practically dragging them on the floor. I don't bother closing my door behind me, I make it to the foot of the bed and fall face first – crawling slowly up the mattress to the pillows. A chuckle pulls my attention to the door, I turn over and lift my head slightly to find Deacon leaning against the frame with a sad smile.

"Come here," I say as I shuffle over a little, making room for him. He doesn't need to be told twice as he closes the distance between him and the bed. Becoming airborne instantly, I can't stop the laugh as he bounces on it, and I'm thrown from my spot.

"Dammit Deacon," I shout as I hit the mattress again and my already tired body twinges everywhere from the impact. He smiles softly then moves himself a little further back on the bed, putting distance between us which hurts my heart.

"I'm so mad at you," I say. I watch the guilt spread across his face, as he moves to climb off the bed. I wrap my hand around his wrist stopping him. He turns wide eyes on me filled with shock.

"I may be mad, but you have to understand, Deacon. What he did to me that day was all about power and I thought we had something more than that?"

"We do."

"Then instead of doing things like that to get your own payback, why don't you try talking to me? If I don't know what you're feeling, how am I meant to know what to do?" His eyes downcast with a sigh, and I hear a deep rattle in his chest. I panic, pulling him closer still – I climb on top of him so I'm straddling is hips. His head whips up and his hands take ahold of my hips.

"We have to use words. Don't do something to me out of revenge or spite." I feel my lower lip wobble as the tears pool in the corners of my eyes. God, today has put me through the ringer. His hand wraps around my neck pulling me onto his chest.

"I am so sorry for what I did," he breathes heavily as his hand runs up and down my spine. "I do love you." I smile, as I feel my lids become heavier as sleep takes me.

"I love you too, Rocket."

CHAPTER TEN

KYLO

My knee bounces up and down as I look around the quad looking for them, my eyes scan the area every few seconds, so I don't miss them. I was surprised when they left after the fight with the nerdy looking one. I was surprised he was the one who had the balls to come at me, and I have to admit he does pack a punch. But I wanted to see firsthand the fieriness that comes with the one and only Bo Walker. She caught the attention of the brother I didn't know I had until a year ago. Then I started searching for him and I found all the things he had done in newspaper articles for the town and then, lo and behold, I find a funeral announcement for him.

A handful of the student body smiled at me this morning as I walked through the grounds, while others threw daggers my way. I nod to a couple of the jocks who nodded their heads and gave me a fist bump. I managed to have a conversation with them after the situation and they were all too willing to give me the lowdown on what's been going on around here recently.

"Hey! Your Kylo right?" a bubbly voice says to my right side, but I don't bother replying.

"Well, you're just as rude as him, then, aren't you. Just so you know, asshole, I'm queen bee of this school." I turn my head to find a blonde dressed like a slutty Stepford wife with a thick layer of crap across her face.

"Oh really?" I scoff at her. "And you are?" I roll my hand hoping like hell she hurries up and then fucks off.

"My name's Tiffany Weinstein. Nice to meet you." Her voice is so high pitched, I clench my teeth with enough force to feel pain in the back of my jaw. What is it with the female population in this school?

"Any reason why you've decided to come over here and bug me?" I snap with a lift brow.

"Well, I…Um." She shuffles from foot to foot, eyes scanning the area for someone to help her. I have to bite my lip to stop laughing as I see some of the students divert their gaze. Yeah, they already know who will rule this school. "Look you don't like the bitch as much as me, if yesterday was anything to go by," she snarls with venom, I look her over, taken back by the hostility and the balls she's showing at the minute.

"I want to make her pay for everything," she says with a savage smile, and I return it with one of my own. Yes, I think she could be of use to me.

An engine roars into the lot pulling my attention from the blonde, the screech of wheels follows the black Camaro that slams to a stop in the empty spot. Damn whoever that car belongs to is my kind of people…*What the fuck*?

I manage to keep my cool as Bo steps out of the driver's side. Almost white hair scraped back into a ponytail. I can see from here the dark make-up around her eyes and the bright red lips she's sporting and damn, I have to admit I can see why he liked her. She's gorgeous. But that's the only thing she is, a pretty package with a rotten core. The others pile out of the truck, eyes scanning the area. I rise to my feet pulling the girl who is still standing in her spot, eyes narrowed on them. I wrap my arm around her neck, so my arms slung across her shoulder almost. I pull her into my side – her head snaps to mine, I wink and a smirk tips my lips when she smiles.

Together we watch them stride across the campus, eyes looking around them as she keeps her eyes forward. A resting bitch face firmly in place, whatever her name is giggles, and my head snaps down to her and she winks.

"Yeah, I agree babe, she's such a toxic bitch," she says with a nasty smile. My eyes connect with Bo's – I notice the glare as they get closer to us.

"Oh, look it's the tramp and her walking STD's," I chuckle seeing the murderous looks from the guys.

"What was that?" the one I know is called Knox snarls stepping closer to us, I feel the blonde tense under my arm. Yeah, I know of him, everyone around here says he's the one you don't want to cross.

"Easy there, marshmallow," I say moving the blonde out of the way and stepping up to him. We're almost the same height, he has a little bulk on me but that doesn't mean anything. "You don't want to be biting off more than you can chew now do you?" I dust imaginary lint of the shoulders of his blazer, with a smirk on my face.

I have to fight to hold in the laugh as he goes bright red in the face – his whole body vibrates with rage. I see his shoulder twitch and I dodge to the side – avoiding the punch to the jaw he's just tried to land on me. I counter with one of my own that clips his jaw and he wildly throws another. I laugh darkly as I evade his poorly timed attacks – laughing my ass off as I dance out of the way. Well, until the other two join in to try and block my path.

"Enough!" My head snaps to the side and my eyes connect with hers. Her face is stoic, like an impenetrable piece of metal.

"He's insignificant," she says looking between the others. "Don't lower yourself to his standing."

"Ouch," I laugh. "What's the matter, baby, do I ruffle them pretty little feathers of yours?" I say with a purr, she lifts a brow and looks down her nose at me – my teeth grind together at the look of disgust on her face.

"This is our town, Kylo." She says down the length of her pert little nose. "Our school. I understand you'll be feeling lost, not knowing where you fit here. But keep in mind you will never be your brother." My nostrils flare as I grind my molars harder. "So, do yourself a favor and stay out of our way or you'll learn the lesson he did."

"Ha! Enlighten me," I say with a sharp tone. "What lesson did you teach my brother?"

"A queen can take a king."

CHAPTER ELEVEN

BO

W ith one last look at him, I walk off leaving Wankstein standing there with her mouth hanging open. Kylo glares at me, but I pay him no mind – I can feel his eyes burning into the back of my head as we make our way through the academy. I've got a meeting with the guidance counsellor this morning, that's more than likely to take up my entire morning. But it beats sitting in a classroom, and listening to the gossip mill.

"You sure about this?" Axel says pulling me to a stop. My eyes drop to the connection of his hand on my wrist, I take a deep inhale – filling my lungs with as much air as I can.

"This needs to be done, keep your eyes open and if things start to look like they're about to spiral, do what you need to," I say with a soft smile. I rise onto my toes and plant a soft kiss on his lips, and he takes that as an invitation. His arm snaking around my back to pull me closer – I laugh as I push him back and he pouts.

"Woah!" Rafe chuckles. "Stop hogging the merchandise." He pulls me free, dropping a quick kiss on my forehead and then just as quickly releases me. Knox steps into his place, I peak around his size to see Rafe eyeing up Axel, and he notices me – I wink as I see pink tinge his cheeks. He growls, gnashing his teeth at me and I burst out laughing. Knox frowns as I shake my head – bringing my attention back to him. I see the unease practically rolling off him, I run my hands up his strong arms until my hands are on his shoulders. I quirk a brow, a little challenge gleaming in my eyes. He scoffs and yanks me forward by the back of my neck, he kisses me with a brutality that takes my breath away. He lets go and steps to the side with a dark look on his face – my core clenches at the look because I know that means one thing. When we get some alone time, I'm going to be walking funny for a while.

Deacon steps into my space then, a soft look on his face as he pulls me into a hug – dropping a kiss on top of my head. "You'll be fine," he says. "Just don't take any of her shit, ok?" I nod my head and he drops a soft kiss to my lips – this throws me off a lot, with how he can switch from the commanding guy I see all the time in the bedroom to the sweet hot nerd I fell for in the beginning.

With one last look, we break off and go our own ways, the guys heading off to their classes. The bell sounds as I head down the hallway where Ms. Clarke's office is situated. The halls are quieter now. The students left lingering had to run to their classes – so, thankfully, I didn't hear any musings from them.

"Shit's about to hit the fan." A voice catches my attention and I stop – hidden behind the pillar, I can hear a couple of people breathing behind it.

"Duh! You think, dude? What are we going to do?" Another says, and I feel my feet freeze in their place.

"I don't give a shit, but like hell is she going to keep her fucking crown. Not after everything before the break." My fists clench at my sides, I should've known she would be the one

causing shit. I manage to unstick a foot to move forward a little – I peak round the corner and lo and behold: Jade and one of the girls from Titan's old crew are standing there.

"Miss Walker!" A voice pulls me out of the spell, and both of them jump out of their skin as I hear Ms. Clarke's heels click against the floor, heading in my direction. "You're aware our meeting started ten minutes ago?"

"I'm aware," I say flicking my eyes to her for a split second – then, I turn my attention back to the other side of the pillar to find their spots now empty. I growl as I turn my attention back to the guidance counsellor.

"Well thanks for that, I wanted to know what else they had to say," I snap coldly. She takes a step back at the hostility, she must be able to feel it rolling off me in waves.

"You sure you're ok for this meeting today?" she enquires with a slight tremble to her voice.

"Not really, but either you or the dean are going to be on my ass after yesterday. So, I'm here let's get this over with."

Her voice becomes like a whiny noise that grates on my nerves. My arse hurts as I try to shift myself on the seat. But the faux leather squeaks under me as I move slightly – I roll my eyes as I pray for the ground to open and swallow me whole.

"Can we go back to the question you spectacularly avoided earlier?"

"Not really but I can see you're going to give it the good ol' college try, aren't you?" Sarcasm is thick in my voice as I pick at my nails, playing off that the topic is putting me on edge.

"How are you feeling about Kylo being here?" she asks with a soft tone. Subtlety isn't really her strong suit. Honestly, I half expected the dean to pull me in and start fishing for answers. I should've known she would get roped in.

"It is what it is," I say with a shrug looking out the window at the greying sky, I watch as the clouds roll. "Looks like rain."

She looks over her shoulder out the window – grunting as the clouds darken the sky further. "Nice change of topic, but you're not getting out of it as easily this time." She says with a little more bite to her tone than usual. "Do you think there is going to be issues now he's here or do you think you can get on?"

"As long as he stays out of my business, Ms. Clarke, everything will be peachy," I say with a sickly sweet smile on my face. My eyes narrow on her as she glares right back at me. Oh, this is definitely different from the oh-so-helpful teacher.

"This is going to cause chaos within the school, Bo. Don't you see this?" she snaps with a clipped tone. I lift a brow - I do like the woman, but this is starting to piss me off. I push to my feet, glaring down at her as she stays in her seat behind the desk.

"You know nothing of what's going on here!" I bellow, my anger getting the better of me this time. "None of you know what I've had to deal with since the so-called king of this town did what he did. Or how I feel after having Frost die. I know he was a bastard a lot of the time, but he tried to make up for it in the end and he died!"

"So, if you want to sit there and lecture me about shit, then be my guest but I won't listen to a fucking word you say." My chest heaves as I try to control myself but seeing the wide-eyed look on her face grates on me. I pull my phone out and check the time, just as the bell for lunch screeches through the area. "Looks like our time's up."

I grab my bag and head out the door, breathing a sigh of relief as the office is left behind me. I fire off a text to the group chat, telling the guys to meet me at the cafeteria – Rafe's reply is instant with a thumbs up emoji followed by a heart. The others send me their weird emojis and I have to chuckle, their personalities are so different, but it works for us.

"How's your boyfriend, hope he's not too sore after not hitting me earlier." My limbs freeze – my head whips up, my attention on the person blocking my way down the corridor. The hall is almost empty as everyone will be in the cafeteria now.

"What do you want Kylo?" I ask with a bored tone.

"I want to speak to the person responsible for ruining my whole life," he growls, stepping closer to me. I stand my ground not backing up like I want to.

"I haven't ruined your whole life," I retort with a huff. "I didn't even know who you were until yesterday."

"Yes, you did, you've seen me before yesterday." He purrs with a smirk. "You saw me outside the coffee shop. When you came out of Frost Enterprise, and the time you went underwear shopping. FYI nice bod, by the way," he winks.

"They thought I was going nuts because of you," I accuse – my nostrils flare. "Why would you stalk me?" I demand.

"You need to know the enemy to destroy them."

"I don't know where you get your hatred for me, Kylo, but your brother tried his best to make amends for the shit that went down between us at the hands of your so-called father." Guilt fills me as I think of what his life might have been like growing up, but then finding out that your brother, you didn't know about, is dead is one way to fuck someone up.

"He's dead because of you and the sperm donor has dropped off the face off the earth because of you. You got everything from his downfall, and I have nothing," he roars, spit flying everywhere. "I want what is mine."

"This is ridiculous," I snap losing my patience with him.

Yes, I know he's confused and everything else. "Your brother was lost, if you don't believe me – you can ask his friends what he was like and what happened."

"You mean the ones you're fucking?" his eyes filled with rage. I get lost in them, though, as they are just like his, and my heart clenches painfully in my chest.

"The only thing I want from them, or you, is to watch your world burn," he snaps – he shoulder checks me as he takes off down the hallway. I watch him go – this is going to end one way or another and I don't like that.

"What the fuck was that!" Axel bellows as he rushes towards me. His face is lined with anger as he glares behind me, I look back over my shoulder but he's not there anymore. I'm pulled into a solid chest as arms wrap around me with a heavy weight.

"He's a lost boy who blames me for the shit show of his life," I say with a shrug – the venom he had doesn't bother me, but what does is how alive I felt with him being a dick. I know that stems from his brother but fuck me, it was intense.

"You don't seem worried about him," he says with a soft voice.

"I'm not, at the moment. He seems to be lashing out where he can but that's it. Now, Jade is going to be a problem I think."

His brows hit his hairline, I take his hand in mine and lead us to the cafeteria – telling him what I heard while on my way to the office. He growls every now and then but agrees we need to keep an eye on her. That won't do anything to stop her, and I need to remind her, again, what I am capable of because clearly the cooler to the face wasn't warning enough.

We make it to the cafeteria with time to grab something, and as soon as I sit between Deacon and Knox, Rafe clicks his fingers and one of the waiters comes running over with a plate. I chuckle as a burger and fries is put in front of me and the

RETURN TO BLACK FROST ACADEMY

server pulls a face. What is with people looking at me weird when I chow down like a starving man? Food is life.

"Hey, I've got to dip out, my uncle wants to see me for something," Axel says as he kisses my temple. I nod - unable to speak because of the food in my mouth. He laughs as he heads out of the room, the others shuffle a little closer and we watch the room.

The bell sounds, and the students get up like brainwashed individuals as we make our way to our next classes. I've got business studies next, which a good thing since the guys are in there with me – so, it's likely to suck a little less. I just hope things begin to settle down.

CHAPTER TWELVE

I head off to the bathroom, before I have to sit my arse down in my psychology class – I really need to drop this shit, since she was the one who picked it for me. I stick my head through the door, straining my hearing to see if any of the cubicles are occupied. After a minute, I know it's clear, and I step inside. Making my way over to the sink, I turn the cold tap and splash water on my cheeks. My face is pale, my breathing rapid as I take slow deep breathes to calm my racing heartbeat.

"Are you going to talk to me about that day?" My head whips up to find Knox throwing daggers my way through the mirror. I quirk a brow, my eyes on him through the mirror – he stands there watching me with his arms folded across his chest. The thick muscle straining the material of his blazer.

"I said we would talk about it at a later date," I say, keeping my back to him. "Can we please talk about this another day?"

"No!" he demands, "No more running, Bo, we need to have this shit out, now," he growls. I watch him through the mirror, and he turns his back on me. He walks over to the door and turns the lock, the sound of it like a clap of thunder – he turns to face me with determination on his face

"You're seriously going to block me in here until I talk to you?" I yell, my frustration is growing as he nods his head in reply. "Knox, get a grip. We're at school and need to go to classes."

"I don't give a fuck about classes. I need to get this shit sorted," he booms, his voice echoing of the tiled walls, "Don't you get it, beautiful," he says stepping closer, "it's been driving me insane."

"You convinced the guys I was going crazy," I growl pushing him back a step. "You were the one to push them to agree that I needed professional help."

My hands tremble as tears pool in my eyes, I've been trying so hard to keep a lid on the swirl of emotions, but the lid is rattling. My chest rises and falls rapidly as I look over his shoulder keeping my eyes on the exit. "You didn't believe me." My chest tightens, admitting it out loud is hard.

"I know, I shouldn't have questioned you. But you have to understand it seemed out there," he says, the anger that was on his face has turned to guilt. "We were losing you! What don't you get when I said to you if you go, we all do."

"That's fucking bullshit," I snap. "When have you ever known me to lie," I demand moving closer. "I've been straight up since I got here, I met you all head-to-head for the shit you pulled. I told you I wouldn't back down." My heart pounds as the emotions run wild within me, my hands are violently shaking. "Did I lie?"

"No, you didn't but fucking hell babe," he growls pushing towards me. "You weren't eating, hardly sleeping. Waking up hysterical when you did sleep and then you said you were seeing someone who is dead." I wince as the words feel like a phantom hand, slapping me across the face. *I am so fucking sick of hearing those words!*

I walk up to him, my head craning as I look up from my

90

small height compared to his, his eyes shine as he breathes heavily. "Move out of my fucking way," I growl as I try to sidestep him.

"No," he growls right back, and every time I try to move around him he blocks my path.

"Fucking move," I roar pushing against his chest forcing him back a step, my anger is building as this continues and I really don't want to be exploding here.

"Not a fucking chance," he snarls, pushing me back with his huge size. "Fucking give me something babe, you've been so collected I don't know how you feel."

"You don't want to see what's boiling under the surface," I snap, faking a step to the left and rush around him to the right. My hand grabs the door knob, when a hand wraps around my throat from behind, he spins me around and away from the door. The sound that leaves me is animalistic as the emotions explode.

"Show me," he booms pushing me further away from the exit, the resounding crack echoes off the tiles as a red handprint grows on his cheek. His eyes widen, then narrow. The look is predatory as he rumbles deep within.

I scream in frustration, my fists pounding on his chest, he wants to see how this has made me feel – fuck it. I punch him in the shoulder pushing him back as I advance again, a twisted smile curls his lips as I land another blow. My chest is heaving as I continue to lose myself to the chaos within. "You didn't believe me," I screech, as I hit him in the stomach doubling him over from the power. "I thought I was going crazy, and you kept pushing instead of speaking to me."

"I love you," he roars, pushing me against the cubicles. "Don't you get that. When you hurt, I do, too. Everything you feel, I feel it just as harshly because I love you that fucking much that I don't want to see you hurting."

I stare at him with my mouth open in awe at his admission, and his lips crash down on mine with a savage brutality that pulls a moan out of me. He pushes forward pressing me into the cubicle as our lips dance. The rumble in his chest has heat shooting to my core. I grip the back of his neck tighter, trying to connect us as one. He breaks the kiss with a smack, my chest heaving as he pulls back to look at me – his hand wraps around my neck holding me in place, I smirk up at him as his eyes darken.

"Do you see?" he rumbles, I push against his hold to get closer, which has a smile spreading across his face as he lunges forward, our lips finding each other. His free hand skims down my side, making me shudder as he moves his hands behind me, grabbing my arse. I moan again, feeling the edges of his lips tip up – he smacks my arse, the sound echoing off the walls as I yelp. He moves his other hand, the pressure releasing off my neck as he lifts me, my legs wrapping around his waist. The hand wraps around my neck again forcing me back, breaking the kiss as I pant – his eyes are alive with mischief.

"Don't take your eyes off me," he commands, I groan, my head trying to roll to the side with my excitement.

"Knox we're in the school bathroom," I pant, and he quirks a brow. Yeah, that protest didn't sound convincing to me either, and he waits to see if I say anything else. I smirk with his eyes on me, and my excitement has soaked my underwear. I hear the sound of a zipper, eagerness filling me, and my underwear is pushed to the side. The nail of his thumb scraping against the bundle of nerves, shocking me with a jolt.

I moan at the sensation, and he slams into me – I open my mouth to scream, but he covers it with his free hand as he pounds into me. The guttural sounds I'm making echo off the tiled walls, as sweat begins to coat the nape of my neck. Knox's moans only spur me on as his hips pick up a punishing pace.

The wood behind me groans like it's about to give way at any moment, and I don't give a shit – the feeling of ecstasy is immense. Sparks fire off in my body as I feel the start of the orgasm build.

"Fuck, fuck, fuck," I chant like a prayer, the feel has my core clenching. As I grip his length with my inner walls, he groans.

"Oh my god," he moans. "If you keep that up, I'm going to cum."

"Fuck me harder," I command. The orgasm building at a rapid pace, I think it's going to tear me apart, but I welcome it. Knox snarls a savage sound as he fucks me harder, my breaths are short gasps as the air is stolen from my lungs. Black dots dance in front of my eyes as the cliff top comes into my mind, I rock my hips meeting him thrust for thrust. The movement ramps up the sensation pushing me over the edge as I detonate. My veins burn with ecstasy as I fall screaming over the edge, a roar joins in as I feel him swell.

Together we cum, as the aftershocks buzz in my body. My legs shake against his arse as I try to bring myself back to reality.

"You ok, gorgeous?" he groans as he unseats himself, and my core clenches at the emptiness.

I giggle as I open my eyes to find him staring at me in concern. "I was enjoying the bliss then," I say with a quirked brow. His eyes widen, then he barks out a laugh – unhooking my legs from behind him. I brace myself to crash to the floor like a heap. But he lowers me gently onto shaky legs, pulling my underwear back into position.

"Seriously?" I question, folding my arms as I lean back to keep myself steady. "You do realize the evidence of what we've just done is going to escape don't you?"

"Good I want people to see it," he says with rumble. "But

make no mistake, gorgeous, I think they already do from your screams." My cheeks heat, as I realize he's right.

I straighten my uniform, grabbing my phone out of my pocket, shocked that it didn't fall out. I notice the time.

"Shit! We really need to get going," I grouse, grabbing my stuff and double checking my reflection to make sure I'm presentable.

"After you," he says with a huge grin on his face.

CHAPTER THIRTEEN

"What do you mean, he's been talking with people to get them on his side?" I ask the jock who came to speak to Knox. He came over all sheepish looking around him, as if he was worried someone would see.

"He's been pulling randoms to the side and having talks with them. He's also had a party each night and a lot of the student body went." He replies his eyes darting everywhere like he's worried someone is spying on us.

I should've known he was up to something, for someone saying they want to end me he's kept his distance. The guy and Knox get lost in a conversation, they're both so animated they haven't realized their talk is taking them further away - but I pay them no attention. My mind trying to figure out what he's up to. I pace in a circle as my mind conjures up all the different things he could be planning, some of them are out there but you never know what that blood line is capable of.

"Bo, look out," someone shouts, my head whips around – Deacon's charging at me with his eyes wide. I spin around just as the screech of a firework is heard, the object coming my way. I run like a bat out of hell, it explodes behind me. As yells fill the air, another screech rings out. My eyes widen as another fire work heads my way. *Motherfucker*! I manage to dive out of the way of this one. Through the smoke I see around six of the wannabes chasing after two guys who jump into the back of a truck, peeling out of the lot with their tires smoking. I pull myself back to my feet, dusting off the bits of mud that landed on me from the impact. A body slams into me throwing me forward from the impact. I only just manage to keep myself upright, I round finding Deacon wide eyed – chest heaving as he looks over me frantically.

"Are you ok?" he croaks as he continues to pull and tug at me to find injuries.

"For fuck sake get off me I'm fine," I growl. "It's not the first time I've had to dodge fireworks – it was a regular occurrence back home."

"What the fuck, babe? Who the hell was that?" he asks as we hear yells and the sound of pounding feet that have me turning around to see Knox charging our way.

"I'm fine," I yell over to him because if he hits me it will feel like I've been hit by a freight train. The screech of tires, has me turning to the parking lot, two cars peel out with the guys chasing after the others in the front seats with a couple of other people, I think. I can't really see that well from this distance. Thank God he slows down, finally jogging over.

"I'm fine but I need you to find out what the fuck that was about," I shout over, and he nods his head. Taking off in the direction he just came, he grabs hold of the jock he was just speaking to. I look over myself seeing bits of soil still on my uniform. I growl as I brush them off seeing mud on my palms.

"What's bugging you?" My eyes connect with his and I feel like the weight on my shoulders is a little less with them around. I blow out a breath, the feeling of frustration seems to be a permanent thing for me at the moment. He's not doing the things I expected – he's a lot sneakier than I would've thought, and this stunt only proves it.

"He's not doing what we thought he would?" I say with a frown – Deacon pulls me closer. Tucking me into his side, dropping a kiss on my temple, I move in even closer, trying to stick myself to his side and pull the strength from him that I know is pulsing in his veins.

"That's because we made the mistake of thinking he would be like his brother," he says with a harsh breath – the words almost whistle through his teeth.

"He's sneakier and more spiteful than Frost was and that's saying something." I bark a laugh because truer words have never been spoken. "Are you sure you're ok?"

"Deacon I'm fine, will you stop fussing," I say between gritted teeth. "Before you say it, I'm not going home."

"Bo," he says, I turn to him, my brow quirked. Like fuck am I leaving because if it does have something to do with this fucker, he will think he's won if I leave.

"What have you got next?" he asks as we watch Knox and the guy continue their heated discussion.

"I've got a free period, I've booked a room in the library to catch up on some of the stuff I need to make up from last term and also see if I can find out what I've just missed." I say with a smirk, tipping the edges of my lips. He eyes me suspiciously, but after a beat of me not clarifying anything for him, he nods – I turn myself a little, kissing him quickly. I pull away as he tries to pull me back into his arms. I smirk as he growls. "Meet you back at the house?" I know he's not got anymore lessons now, but this is something I agreed on with the dean; that I would use a free period to study so he knows that I'm not falling behind. He nods again, as I walk backwards towards the building with a huge grin on my face.

The odd few people smile or say "hi' as I pass them, or

ask if I'm ok. I trudge my way up the stairs to the bathroom, since I didn't get chance to do what I needed to when Knox disturbed me earlier. There is one on the lower floor but, honestly, it's disgusting to say this place is for rich people – and I'm not putting myself at risk of catching something. It wasn't too bad when I had a dorm, I'd just take my ass back to my room and do what I needed to but now I walk the flight of stairs to the bathroom there as it's hardly used.

"Your boy's still salty, is he?" A voice says, my head whips around to find the owner whom I know is lurking, but the corridor is empty. "What's the matter, princess, didn't know this place as well as you thought you did?" Kylo steps out of an alcove I've never noticed before, I narrow my eyes at him and he smirks, stepping closer to me.

"Back off," I snarl. How do I always seem to find myself alone with him at inconvenient times? The guys are going to flip their shit. "Guess you're another one with stalker tendencies, then," I snort. "It must run in the family."

"What the fuck's that supposed to mean?" he snarls, grabbing the front of my blazer pulling me closer.

"Your dad turned out to be the stalker that was terrorizing me, even when I lived in the UK." I growl, with a menacing sound – but it doesn't unnerve him like it does most people. The smirk turns into a full all-teeth smile. "Then he got all murder-y close to the end, so yeah it definitely runs in the family. Nice touch with the fireworks by the way," I say with a wide smile like I'm impressed.

"I don't know what the fuck your talking about. What is it about you that has all the men in my family wanting to have you as theirs?" he muses rubbing is thumb across his bottom lip. My eyes are unintentionally drawn to the movement. "You see something you like, princess?" my head snaps up and my eyes connect with his – I'll never get used to his eyes being the same as his.

"Nope, it's just a little freaky that you're both so similar," I say with a snort. "One of him was a test, two of him is the world having a laugh at my expense."

"How so?" he questions, while winding the loose strand of hair around his finger, he steps into me now, so we are chest-to-chest. Well, touching, since there is a noticeable size difference between us.

"It's like a pearl." He rubs the hair between his fingers, staring at the color intently. My teeth grind together, I yank the hair out of his grasp and tuck it behind my ear.

"You planning on sniffing me like a dog too?" I snap, losing my patience with this, but I'm a little pissed as my bladder screams at me and I fidget.

"You make me chuckle with that fire you have. I bet we would be good together if you weren't a whore," he says with his arms folded across his chest. I can see the definition through the material as it tries its best to hold the arms within it.

"Whore? Me?" I bust out laughing. Does he really think the name calling is going to bother me? I've heard so much worse over the years. Fucking hell these people need to give their heads a shake. "Wow, that's so original. So what if you think I'm a whore? Is that meant to affect me in any way?" His brows shoot up towards his hairline.

"You really think the words of a lost boy is going to bring me to my knees?" I scoff, his eyes narrow and he takes another step back. I take this as my chance, I move closer a fraction, and he backs up again. "I've been through more shit than you know, Kylo. This shit you're trying, at the moment, is getting old very quickly. So, I will say this again. I am not to blame for your brother's death." I don't give him a chance to respond. With a filthy look up and down him so he can see my feelings for him, I take off towards the bathroom, because, between us, I'm half a second away from pissing my pants.

The water runs as I wash my hands, and I look at my reflection in the mirror. I've never looked as tired as I do now – my eyes are thickly circled with black bags. My eyes look bloodshot, my hair has lost some of the shine, and I look grey. To everyone else I look fine, but I know things are starting to take their toll on me. The board of trustees are still being dicks about wanting me to bail them out – but, as they said, we were never married, so what happens to them is nothing to do with me. But then that's the question I've asked myself repeatedly, why hasn't Kylo taken over the reins of it and the finances that come with it? Why is he so dead set on taking everything that is mine when he can have what's rightfully his?

"Oh, look it's the home-wrecker." Wankstein strolls into the bathroom with a nasty smile on her face. I grab a paper towel drying my hands as I keep eye contact with her through the mirror.

"Do all you arseholes have a homing beacon on me or something?" I say with a chuckle. "Because you all seem to keep finding me even when I don't want you to."

"Yeah, well I want you out of my school, bitch," she says with a command. Her eyes narrow on me as she looks me up and down like a piece of shit. "You killed the love of my life, and I will watch you burn for it."

"How can he be the love of your life when he married me?" I snap losing my temper with her. Her eyes widen as she gasps. *So, she doesn't know it was a fake wedding then? Interesting.*

"You were a means to an end for them, I told you to know your worth but you're so desperate for a false power it blinds you."

"I.." her words break off, and her lower lip trembles as I see the tears begin to pool in her eyes. I turn to face her, her hands shake as I glare at her. I pull myself up on the sink unit – looking at her properly. Dark shadows line under her eyes and the curves she once had are flat. I can see shadowing on the lower half of her neck that disappears under her shirt.

"Let me guess," I say canting my head to the side. "Daddy dearest was pissed at you for losing Frost, so he's been beating you since the day it happened?" Her eyes nearly pop out of her head as her mouth opens and closes like a fish out of water. "I don't particularly like you Wankstein, but no one should go through that sort of thing."

She continues to stare at me for a couple of seconds. Then she takes off out of the door - but not before I see the tear carve a track down her cheek. I feel a little bad for her, because after meeting her father at the society meeting, I can understand why she so desperately tried to keep her claws in him. My phone pings, I pull it out to find a message in the group chat of Rafe saying he had stopped by the library to tell me he will be home late tonight as he has training, and to make sure I was ok after the stunt. I check the time and *shit!* Half my free period is nearly gone. I grab my stuff and fire off a quick message telling him I'm ok and I'll see him at home.

Just as I step out of the bathroom a high-pitched scream fills the air, I rush out into the stairwell – horrified as I watch Wankstein roll down the stairs like a ragdoll. I look for the anyone else but we're the only ones here. I rush down the stairs to find her screaming and bloody at the bottom in a heap.

"What happened?" I ask, trying to work out where the blood is coming from. "I heard a noise and then I was rolling," she screams, tears stream down her cheeks.

"You're saying someone pushed you?" I ask disbelief clear in my tone. There wasn't anyone else here. I look, but nothing.

Her screams attract the attention of the other students that are milling around, I tell them to get a teacher. As I place her bag under her head, I don't want to touch her. I know moving her would be a very silly mistake, at the moment, as her leg is bent in a weird direction.

"Tiffany, can you hear me," I ask her as her eyes flutter closed. "Tiffany, I need you to stay awake," I command her – I breathe a sigh of relief as her eyes snap open with a start.

"You called me by my name?" she says with a look of shock – a chuckle passes my lips as I see the confusion on her face. "Yeah, well don't take it for me starting to like you," I say with another laugh. She laughs with me, a slice of fear washes over me as she coughs and blood comes out of her mouth.

"What happened," Mr. Mathieson the English studies teacher bellows as he rushes in. I explain what I saw, as the crowd of students gets thicker behind us.

"Has someone called the ambulance?" he asks, and I nod my head to the nerd with the phone pressed to his ear. "Are you sure she was pushed?" he asks, with a pale white expression. He looks around with suspicion clear on his face.

"She said she was pushed," I say. "I heard her scream as I came out of the bathroom. But I didn't see anyone else around."

Loud voices pull both our attention away from the conversation as paramedics push through the students. I step back out of the way to give them the space they need to treat her, I look up to the top of the stairs again. Trying to look for something I may have missed the first time – but nothing is there.

"What happened?" Knox bellows pushing through the crowd as he makes his way towards me with terror on his face.

When his eyes connect with mine – I see his shoulders relax, the tension that was there now gone.

"I heard her scream and saw her rolling down the stairs," I say quickly to explain before I crash into Deacon's chest – since he pulled me off my feet as soon as he saw me.

They pull me away from the chaos, the crowd descends again trying to push closer as we move outside, and the other students press closer to the madness. The paramedics can be heard yelling at everyone telling them to move back – the guys crowd me looking me over like I'm the one who fell. The sound of sirens wailing in the distance, have us all looking to the carpark entrance just as the police come flying through the gates. The noise quiets as they make their way over – asking the paramedics questions as they lift her onto the trolley. Her scream of pain has me wincing as I watch as the students, move further away from the scene now.

"Bo?" a young officer says to me as he eyes the guys a look of fear slips across his face – his adam's apple bobs in his throat and then it's quickly gone.

"The paramedics said you were the one to find her. Can you come with me I have some questions." He says, motioning for me to enter the empty room with the door open. I move forward, when Deacon halts me.

"You can ask her the questions here," he snarls, the officer takes a step back – fear once again on his face.

"Ok fine. Can you tell me what happened?"

"I came out of the bathroom and heard her scream, I rushed to the noise to find her rolling down the stairs. I rushed down to help her and she said she'd been pushed." I tell him with a sigh, I don't know how many more times I have to repeat myself. His pen scratches at the paper as he takes notes on our conversation the noise gates in me.

"Is that everything?" Knox snaps from my side, he's been

standing there listening to me recount what happened, again. The presence of him behind me was a welcome relief to the stress that is running through my veins. I didn't tell them about our run-in in the bathroom because nothing really happened, and they wouldn't believe me.

"We're done. Thank you, Miss Walker and I want to offer my condolences for the loss of your aunt and Frost." I mutter a thank you as I head out into the fresh air once again.

Making my way further away from the loud voices, I feel the guys behind me. Deacon is tapping away on his phone which brings a smile to my lips just from hearing the noise. It doesn't take long for us to get to our cars, and I turn and sit on the front. Sliding myself up so my legs are lifted off the floor – we all watch in silence as they bring out Wankstein and put her in the back of the ambulance. I flick through my socials on my phone waiting to get back to the rest of the day when a hand on my leg pulls my attention away from my phone. Four police officers are standing in front of us with blank expressions on their faces.

"I already answered your colleague's questions," I say, waving them off and turning my attention back to my phone.

"Bo Walker, you're under arrest" one of the men says as he steps closer to me. The guys yell with outrage as the officer turns me around. Cuffs are placed on my wrists as the cold bite of metal has a hiss passing between my teeth.

"You have this all wrong," I demand as I look to the guys – they all stand there red faced with their rage clear.

"You have the right to remain silent." I tune the rest of the words out as I look to my boys. I can see their lips moving, but I hear no words. Pressure on my arms has me looking to the officer behind me and he nods his head. I start walking towards the police car, when numerous voices come crashing in on my ears. My head snaps up to find the majority of the school on the grounds staring at me as I'm frog marched to the police car. I slide in and look back to see the guys arguing and shoving one of the officers – Knox's gaze connects with mine. I shake my head and smile trying to reassure them that everything is going to be alright when the door slams with a deafening sound.

CHAPTER FOURTEEN

AXEL

"I know you're up to something old man," I snarl at my uncle who just smiles at me from his seat behind the desk. Not saying a word – I growl in frustration. I've been here over an hour and all he has done is talk in fucking riddles. Words that don't make sense and gives me the biggest headache ever.

"You look about half a second away from losing your shit, Axel," he says with a chuckle. He fills my glass with another two fingers worth of bourbon – I grab it, throwing it back in one go, welcoming the burn in the back of my throat. "All I can say is there are a lot of things that are moving at the moment, and I need to tread carefully to make sure it doesn't go tits up."

"I've always known you to be an honest man, even though you have zero filter and offend people most of the time. You have never withheld anything from me." My voice echoes throughout the word, with enough force to make him push back away from the desk.

"I…" His words are cut off with a shrill shrieking nose – I glower at him down the length of my nose. "Will you answer your fucking…."

"It's your phone," he states – that's when I feel it vibrating in my pocket. I pull it out with enough force to tear my pocket a little. My eyes widen when I see Knox's name flashing on the screen.

"What's the matter," I snap into the phone. His next words have all the fight leaving me as I drop into the seat opposite my uncle – eyes wide. I listen to everything that's happened while I've been here, and I can't believe it.

"Yeah, I'll get it sorted and meet you as soon as I can," I say, ending the call. My eyes connect with my uncle as he shows concern. My mouth opens and closes as I try to get the words to pass my lips.

"Bo's been arrested," I blurt managing to push the lump aside. My uncle shoots to his feet, outrage as clear as day.

"What happened?" He demands with a booming voice. He grabs his phone from the desk and starts typing like a madman. His fingers flying so fast I can barely track them.

"Weinstein was pushed down a flight of stairs and they arrested Bo thinking she's done it." My voice is low as a mix of emotions passes through me. Things are getting out of hand now.

"Uncle?" I say, his head snaps up to mine- his concentration pulled away from his phone. "She had nothing to do with this. You have to get her out of there." His phone pings with the sound of a notification and I wait for him to tell me how he plans to get her out.

"We can't go throwing money around to get her out," he says with a deflated tone, my brows hit my hairline with shock.

"We need to get her out of there!"

"Things are moving quicker than I thought," he snaps with a curt tone. "I thought we had more time to get the things in place that are needed but I was wrong."

"What the fucking hell are you talking about, you idiot?" I bellow the words as I throw the glass that held the bourbon watching as it smashes against the wall. "You know she's not capable of doing something like that. She pays you for this kind of shit, so do your fucking job."

"I will do my job, but the best thing at the moment is to do things properly!" He snaps back at me.

"Fuck you!" I take off out of the office, my veins thunder with pent up rage as my focus is to get my ass back to the academy and meet the guys so we can go to the station together.

I'm surprised I made it back to the Academy in one piece – I ran every stop light on the way back. Like fuck was I being held up in traffic. The grounds are alive with movement, as students congregate on the grass not bothering to do anything the teachers are telling them. I spot the guys as I pull up - my breathings labored as I jump out of the car, not bothering to turn the engine off.

"What the fuck is going on?" My voice booms catching the attention of not only the guys but the rest of the student body too. They rush over to me, and I can see the rage rolling of Knox in waves. Rafe looks really uncomfortable and on edge. His head whips side to side as he looks around but the look of defeat on his face pulls at the strings on my heart. Deacon taps away on his phone like a madman – obviously trying to figure a way out of this. Rafe dives on me, I only just manage to stop us both from falling in a heap. I chuckle, pulling him into my side and he comes willingly. My head snaps up as I realize we aren't alone, but Deacon is smiling. Our eyes connect and he mouths "*thank you*" to me. I nod my head back to him and then turn my attention to Knox. His eyes are alight, and a smirk tips the edge of his lips.

"About fucking time," he says with a laugh. Rafe jumps back from me then remembering where we are. Whispers break out amongst the crowd – that I quickly shut down with a death glare, with enough venom and a promise of pain. "Does Bo know?"

"She was the one that got them to get it on the night of the wake," Deacon says laughing fully this time. Rafe groans as he looks between his friends, and I chuckle – I told him he wouldn't get any judgement from them.

"Ok back on topic. What did Mr. Geoffrey say?" Unease layers Knox's voice and I have try and swallow the lump in my throat.

"He told us to do things by the book," I say with a low tone forcing them to move closer to be able to hear me. "He won't do what we want him to because apparently things are moving quicker than he anticipated."

"What the fuck does that even mean?" Deacon growls, his face lined with outrage – his fingers fly across the phone. A ping comes through, and he snarls again, his eyes are as sharp as stones.

"He's told us to try and find out who did it." My nose crunches with the lie but I don't care about what the fucker says – we need to find out who is behind it.

"Shall we split up?" Rafe growls I can see the unease rolling off him in waves – it fills the air thickly. I have never seen him this on edge before!

Voices echo throughout the area. The bastards aren't even trying to keep their noise down so we can't hear them. I grind my teeth trying to rein my rage – my hand visibly trembles from the amount of restraint I'm showing. A high-pitched cackle catches my attention – my head whips around so fast I'm surprised my neck doesn't break. Jade stands there with a group of girls who used to run in the school with that Tiffany girl. My strides eat up the ground as I charge over to her – the other girls' eyes widen and mouth open. My hand takes a firm grip around her throat before they have chance to utter a word. Her eyes bulge out of her head as she squeaks.

"What the fuck did you do?" I rumble the timber so deep it rattles in my chest. The whites of her eyes show as she looks at me then, behind me. Her mouth opens but no words are able to make it past.

"Axel?" The words are soothing, I know they've sent Rafe to try and talk me down, but it won't work this time.

"I know you had something to do with this, you little bitch," I boom, pushing her backwards until her back hits the wall with a thump. She groans and I release the hold on her, a little, allowing her to be able to get more air into her lungs. She coughs but keeps her eyes locked with mine – a sultry smile spreads across her face as she looks me up and down.

"I didn't do anything to upset your precious fuck piece," she says with a soft edge to her voice. Her hand runs along my arm that still has a hold of her. "Do you do this to her when you fuck?" she purrs. A cold feeling rushes down my spine as I hear the others behind me growl their annoyance at her. I grind my teeth as I harden my gaze pulling her closer – her eyes dilate with lust as we come nose-to-nose.

"What I do with my girl has fuck all to do with a whore like you," I snap – gnashing my teeth together. "Now tell me what you did!"

Her smile is savage as our gazes clash – the sultry look is replaced with one as sharp as broken glass. "I can be your whore if you want? I know that would hurt oh-so-sweet Bo very much," she says with a low chuckle. "Question, baby, do you think she's still salty after he made her watch?"

"I should snap your fucking neck here and now!" I bellow, my grip tightening – my smile is menacing as I watch the cockiness disappear off her face. "I'm telling you now bitch, If I find out you did this, I will end you myself."

"I had nothing to do with it," she screams in my face – desperation clear. "You know what they're like – they hate each other. How do you know it wasn't an accident," she pleads as I feel her away getting smaller in my grasp.

"Axel!" Knox's voice pulls me out of my madness – my head snaps to the right and our eyes connect. Rage stares back at me from behind his features, his head shakes side-to-side as I look at the jock standing next to him. I drop her – she thumps to the floor with a yell of fear.

"We've got a lead," he says as he pushes the guy forward a step and he takes off jogging towards the jump. We all follow behind – my rage riding me hard, but I will find out who is behind this. For her.

CHAPTER FIFTEEN

BO

"Now, are we going to get this right this time?" The nasally officer says to me from his seat across from me. I quirk a brow as my eyes take in the interrogation room much like the one the others brought me to earlier. They lost patience with me after about an hour of me saying no comment with a wicked smile on my face. Clearly, they've never met a Brit. We can be the most annoying people on the planet and where I come from, you never speak to the police, even if you're innocent. Hopefully, the guys have gotten in touch with Axel and Mr. Geoffrey, and, no doubt, he should be here soon to bail my ass out of here.

"Look this will go easier if you just tell us what happened to Miss Weinstein," the officer says with a snap of his voice. "Did you push her down the stairs?"

"No comment," I say – not bothering to look at him. I can hear his teeth grind as he blows out a harsh breath and I have to fight to hold in the chuckle that's building.

"I know you don't get on and you have had previous run-ins that weren't reported," he says with a smile tipping the edges of his lips. I can see the determined look he has out of the corner of my eye – as well as in the reflection of the two way mirror I'm sat opposite of.

"Let me guess, someone is in there watching this farce as you try to get me to say something?" I ask with a lifted brow – my eyes meet his and I see his widen a fraction. "Who is it? Your sergeant and someone to read my body language, I take it?"

His face flushes a deep red as he tugs on the collar of his shirt. "Listen here, you little bitch!" he snaps his palms slamming on the top of the desk. His eyes narrow on me as he pushes himself closer – his eyes glinting with rage. "You may be the Queen out there, but in here, you do as you're fucking told," he bellows – stray spit landing on the desk.

I lift my chin high with a look of boredom across my face. "Now, who the fuck are you to speak to me like that, you fucking dog's body," I growl with a ferociousness I use when I'm really starting to become pissed.

"Did you push her," he bellows back not heeding the warning I have just subtly given him. I rise to my feet, the chain on the chuffs clinking against each other as I lock eyes with him. I lift a brow and my lips set in a scowl, "No comment."

His face goes from slightly flushed to beet red in a matter of seconds, I chuckle as I imagine steam coming out of his ears – with a roar he grips hold of the front of my blazer pulling me across the desk. My feet not touching the floor, I have to anchor my palms on top of the table to stop myself from toppling to the side.

"I know you pushed my niece," he spits, my chuckles turn to fully on laughter as I realize

he's another one of the arseholes of this town. "Admit it! Admit you were the one who did it."

"You mean, watch her roll down the stairs like a rag-doll?" I say with a bark of laughter. "Yeah, I saw her rolling and go splat at the bottom," I declare with a hint of venom in my voice. "But I wasn't the one to push her."

"You were. You're to blame for everything going wrong in this fucking town," he roars pulling me closer, the desk biting into the fronts of my thighs. Pain radiates up my legs and my toes begin to tingle from the lack of blood flow. "You're a disease on this town."

I try to tug back at the words, my chest squeezes tightly as my mood goes from taunting to war in zero point one seconds flat. "I'm a fucking disease," I spit the words at him. If I was a dog, no doubt my hackles would be up, at this moment in time.

"The people before me were the fucking disease, sucking the life out of everything and making people who didn't have much have to beg for what they wanted." He lets go and I slide back off the desk, my ass hitting the chair. I growl as all the blood rushes back to my legs. "What's the matter PC Plod?" I smirk as he rounds the desk, his hand lifts in the air. "I wouldn't do that if I was you," I sass. "If that connects, I promise you this, I will fuck your world with a blunt edged carving knife."

He jumps back, eyes wide, just as the door crashes open by an older looking gentlemen. His brows are pinched and he looks like he's chewing on a bed of rusty nails. "Detective if you threaten the suspect one more time," his voice booms – forcing me to wince as the noise grates on my eardrums.

"I know this little bitch did it, sir," he spits at his boss. "I know it – just give me a few more minutes and I can get the confession out of her." He pleads with the sergeant who hasn't looked at me once since stepping into the room – if I'm not mistaken that looks to be a sheen of sweat gathering below his hairline.

"Miss Walker, please forgive the imbecile," he says with a soft smile. I look the new person up and down, he throws daggers at the detective to shut him up every time he opens his mouth. "Everything has been processed at the front desk, and you're free to go," he says with an urgent lilt to his voice – I cock my head to the side watching as he quickly unshackles me from my restraints, a smile tipping the edge of my lips as I see the officer's face take on a hint of red in his cheeks.

"What the hell are you doing, boss," the other bellows. He reaches to grab hold of my wrist and I yank back, toppling the chair behind me. I smile at him savagely – he snarls right back, and I chuckle darkly.

"New evidence has come to light," the Sargent states with a clipped tone, and I watch as the shoulders of the detective vibrate with restrained rage.

His head whips back and forth between the pair of us and I let the triumphant gleam spread across my face. He bellows again lunging at me. The sergeant grips him by the collar pulling him close and whispering something into his ear. I try to strain my hearing, but I can't make out what's been said. It must be something though as all the color drains from the detective's face and his chin drops to his chest.

"What do you mean there's new evidence?" I ask, my face pinched in a scowl – the Sargent shuffles from foot to foot.

"You're free to go," he replies not making eye contact with me. I look to the detective, his chin is still on his chest, but I can see the tension in his jaw from him grinding his teeth. I smile and nod at the sergeant heading out of the room as I rub my wrists which have become sore from the cuffs. Whatever you did, Mr. Geoffrey, you're a genius.

The town car pulls up outside the house, and my heart beats erratically in my chest. I honestly thought they would find a bullshit charge and I would be seeing the guys at visitation. I smile as I stand outside my own door, my brain enjoying the tranquility for a moment. My fingers brush the handle when it swings open and a body crashes into me – I bark out a laugh as wide eyes snap to me.

"Oh, my child," Ms. Jeanette squeals with horror mixed with glee. "What are you doing out here?"

"I was taking in the scenery when someone in a hurry barreled me over," I laugh as her eyes widen. "Where are you off to in such a hurry?" My brow lifts as her face flushes pink.

"I was just about to come down to the station and raise hell," she says with a chuckle. It's lucky that they let me out when they did because no way in hell would anyone manage to deal with her when she's pissed. Even the devil himself would shit himself if she was the one to chastise him.

"Well, I really wish I would have gotten to see that, now," I say with a laugh. "I should get arrested again just so I can watch."

"Don't jest child you know what I'm like. The officers wouldn't know what had hit them," she snarls, whacking me on the shoulder. "Well, since you're here now, you can deal with them, and I'll go for a coffee with Angie."

"Oh lord help again in the coffee shop," I say with a chuckle jumping out the way as she tries to hit me again. "Can you behave yourself?" I ask from inside the doorway, and her eyes narrow to slits.

She heads down the front steps and I smirk as an Uber pulls up out front. She slides in giving me a wink and I know, now, she's up to no good. I bet they planned their little secret cocktail hours they think I don't know about. I did offer to buy her a car, but she wasn't having any of it – honestly, I would ask anyone the same thing, but do you want to argue with the woman?

I make my way through the house, and I can hear the guys

arguing in the kitchen – the scent of chicken satay noodles hits my nose, making my mouth water. "You best not be eating my food." I say with a huge grin as I lean against the wall. All of their heads whip around – Rafe nearly unseats himself from the bar stool, and the legs screech against the floor.

"Wow, you trying to deafen me now?" I push off the wall as they all rush over to me. Knox hits me first, he manages to stop me falling, at the last minute, gasping as I fall.

He pulls me into his chest, dropping a kiss on my forehead, as Axel rips me out of his arms and engulfs me in a hug. I untangle myself pushing back slightly so I can see into his eyes. The relief shining back at me has a ball of emotion growing in my chest. "Tell Mr. Geoffrey thanks, the next time you speak to him," I say with a warm smile on my face.

"What are you on about, Majesty?" he says with a deep rumble, and my veins pulse within at the sound as I feel a shot of lust race to my core. I open my mouth to say something, but Rafe cuts me off by diving on me – knocking me to the ground with a thump. He followed me down but stopped all his weight falling on me with his hands. His eyes are alight as he grins at me in that sexy way of his. He drops the tension from his elbows bringing us nose to nose, I feel his warm breath flutter across my cheek. He kisses me quickly on the lips, I moan a little at the small contact.

"Behave yourself, asshole," Deacon snaps pulling him off me – he extends his hand with a stone look on his face. I smile at the grump and take his hand squealing as he pulls me to my feet. "How are you here?"

I look between them, confusion on my face as I see the same confused look shining back at me. "Mr. Geoffrey got me out," I say.

"Majesty?" I turn to Axel, finding a frown on his face as he sides eyes the others. "He told us to do things by the book."

"What're you on about? He got me out," I say with a huff. I'm in no mood for the stupid pranks they play. "The sergeant released me. I thought it had something to do with Mr. Geoffrey?"

"No, Majesty. We tore through the school after he told us to wait, and we couldn't find any leads on who had done it. We haven't been back long, and I was just about to call him again." Axel says with a troubled expression. My mouth opens and closes like a fish as my brain tries to catch up with what the hell is going on.

"The sergeant said new evidence had come to light, and that's why they let me go," I say with a small voice, my confusion clear.

"Do you want me to call him?" Axel asks with a snap of his voice. I can see the vein in the side of his neck throbbing which tells me that he's pissed.

"No, it's ok. I'll find out what's happening tomorrow. What else happened while I was locked up?" I ask, my eyes looking between them all. I see Rafe's complexion pale, and Axel tries to clear a lump form this throat. Deacon barks out a laugh, and Knox smirks. "What happened?"

"Some of the students may have an idea about Axel and Rafe," Deacon says with a cautious tone, I see Rafe deflate at his admission.

"What do you mean?" I ask looking to the pair that look like they want to run right about now.

"Rafe comforted Axel and it looked…" he starts. "Well, you know how it looked. A few of the students saw. Knox threatened a couple of people because of it," he states with a sad look.

"You know?" I ask Knox as I look more closely at his face to try and read him, but as ever it's a struggle. His face is stoic as he looks to his friends who are both turning red.

"I had an idea, but today confirmed it," he says. My eyes narrow as I see a twitch. I turn my back to the others and step closer my eyes turning to slits as I glare at him. That's when I see the corner of his mouth twitching. The little shit, he's enjoying this. I smack him in the shoulder, and he burst out laughing. "Ow! What was that for?"

"Piss off. That didn't hurt, you big baby," I growl. "I saw you start to smirk, you knew, and you let them believe you didn't."

"Okay, Okay. I went to the bathroom at the wake, and I saw you in the doorway – I was going to scare you but then I saw what had your attention" He admits with a wide smile on his face.

"Oh, for fuck's sake," Rafe roars, rushing out of the room with his face flaming. A savage sound fills the room, my head whips to Axel and there's murder in his eyes.

"Rafe, its ok," he bellows after his friend, I hold a hand up to stop Axel from going to war. Knox looks at me with a guilty look. I narrow my eyes at him – hoping my face tells him how pissed I am with him. *Yeah, arsehole you royally fucked up there!*

I'm just about to tell Axel to go after him, but he takes off after him and I'm left standing here with a smiling Deacon and guilty Knox.

"Sorry about the caveman," Deacon says with a smirk as Knox growls. "We'll go out for a bit." They head off to the front door, and I open my mouth to tell them not to go. "He was worried about you. They both were," he says just as he slips through the door – closing it with a wink.

I'm left standing here, how does he always know what people need before they even know themselves? I take the stairs two at a time, as I hunt down two of my boys. I check Rafe's room first, the door bangs against the wall but I find it empty.

Huh? I move a door down and throw Axel's door open and I'm met with the same thing. I move to my room, and I see Rafe on the bed with his head in his hands – with Axel on his knees in front of him.

"Babe, it's ok you know what Knox is like. He's a douche," Axel says to comfort him. I snort a laugh. Rafe's head snaps up and his eyes connect with mine. I smile at him, then look to Axel who is smirking at me over his shoulder. I wink at him, moving closer into the room, I grab the back of the desk chair – wheeling it over until its bedside them at the foot of the bed. I drop down into it, my body thrumming with excitement.

"Kiss him."

CHAPTER SIXTEEN

B oth their brows hit the hairlines as I lean forward my arms on my knees. I smile as they look to each other and then back to me. I can see the unease in Rafe's face, and it kills me. "You heard me." I growl.

"Majesty?" Axel rumbles, another shot of lust going straight to my core. "What're you doing?"

"Exactly what we've wanted to do since that night" I purr, leaning back in my chair – widening my legs. "Rafe this is what you want, show me what you've been dreaming about."

His eyes instantly smolder with lust as he looks at me, I smirk at him then run the tip of my tongue across my top lip. I see the tremble in his shoulders as I bite into the plump flesh, both their eyes flash. I chuckle as Axel lunges forward, connecting his and Rafe's lips with a brutality that has my underwear soaked. Teeth clashes together as they both fight for dominance, and the sight has my hand twitching to relieve the ache in between my legs.

"Put him on his knees, Axel," I rumble, their lips part with surprise, I smile – nodding my head encouragingly. A wide smile spreads across Axel's face as he pushes up until he's standing in front of Rafe. His hand gently grabs the sides of his head, I watch mesmerized as he tugs just a little and Rafe follows willingly – dropping to his knees in front of him.

I lean forward eager to see who is going to make the next move, Rafe looks to me – I bite my bottom lip again. The sound of a belt buckle being undone has my eyes zeroing in on Axel as Rafe unbuckles it – his eyes locked on mine. I nod my head in encouragement and wink at him, he smiles his most adorable smile. I shuffle myself forward as Axel's length springs free, while his hand grips the back of Rafe's head and pushes him onto it. Rafe opens his mouth and Axel pushes in, I groan. Lust roars within me as Rafe's sounds and Axel's moans have me leaning back in the chair.

My legs widen as the tips of my fingers run up the length of my thigh and towards my centre. Rafe gags, while Axel groans deep in his throat – I push the string to the side. My thumb grazing the bundle of nerves, I gasp at the sensation just as Axel rumbles. My head snaps up, our eyes connecting as he watches me circle the nerves with the pad of my thumb.

"Fuck me," I groan, head rolling onto the back of the chair.

"Fuck." Is echoed as both of the guys groan again, I hear the zipper going down and then the scratching of fabric as Rafe's slurps become faster. I lift my head, the sensations on overload in my body, and my eyes widen as I see Rafe with his shaft in his hand – his grip tight as he pumps it in his grip. Swallowing Axel to the end – I jump as a hand brushes against my leg. Axel runs his fingers over my thigh, then back onto the arm of the chair. He grips it pulling it closer, the wheels squeak in protest at the harsh movement.

He grins at me as my eyes stay on Rafe and he leans to the side, his thumb taking over for mine and starts to rub frantic circles. "Mmmm, fuck," I groan. Axel snarls, pulling his length out of Rafe's mouth who yells his protest, though his eyes widen when he sees where the other thumb is, and he licks his lips.

Axel pushes him towards me as Rafe moves around so he's facing me. "Do what you want here," I pant as he licks his lips. "But I want to watch him fuck you while you dine on me." Axel growls again, his hand lashing out he grips the material, tearing it in one go – so I'm fully open to them both now. He pushes Rafe's head to my centre, my head rolls to the side as I moan – as his tongue swipes up through my folds. The sound of a foil packet being ripped echoes throughout the room.

"You ok with this, Rafe?" I ask, his eyes connect with mine – I bark out a laugh as he grins at me.

"Hell yes," he declares, diving in.

My head rolls back, I moan as the flat of his tongue runs up my centre making a shudder pass through me. "Look at me, Majesty."

The command has my eyes snapping open, Axel's dark gaze on me. I watch intently as he rolls the condom down his length. My eyes widen as I see a bottle of something in his hand, he flicks the cap and pours a large amount on his length, and I groan again.

"Oh, aye, where did you pull that from?" I manage to force out between pants. Rafe is eating me out like a starving man. Axel winks, then turns his attention to Rafe's ass lubing him up well. *Oh, shit this is hotter than I imagined.*

Little bolts of sensation fire off in my body as I feel the orgasm start to build, I watch as Axel settles himself properly. Rafe's head snaps up and a guttural moan comes out of him, he thrusts two fingers into me at the same time Axel fully seats himself. All of us moan together as one, "Oh fuck," I pant as Rafe works me over with his fingers and tongue. The sounds of him lapping at me – along with Axel's moans as he pumps into Rafe has me on the edge.

"You want him to fuck you harder?" I purr, running my fingers through Rafe's hair. His nod is instant – but he manages not to break his connection with my pussy. A disturbingly beautiful small spreads across Axel's face as he pulls out and slams into Rafe from behind enough force to push his fingers deeper into me.

"Fuck me," I shout as the sensations take over and I become a huge giant ball of nerves. His moans vibrate against me taking the sensation to whole new heights as the sound of flesh smacking against flesh fills the room.

Axel pistons into Rafe like a man possessed, and I run my tongue across my lip. He snarls savagely at the movement thrusting even harder. My nails are digging into the arms of the chair as the orgasm builds even further, "Fuck, make me cum, babe, please," I beg Rafe as I watch my boys fuck. His fingers pump in and out faster than ever as he nips at the bundle of nerves with his teeth. My head drops back as the violent trembles take over me, "That's it. Keep going," I pant as the cliff edge wobbles beneath me. Axel roars, Rafe moans – he clamps done on my clit, the moan that escapes me as my orgasm explodes is a mix of a guttural sound and scream. He pistons his fingers, lapping at me with the flat of his tongue, carrying me through the aftershocks as the orgasm slowly recedes.

Axel roars again, Rafe moans, and I watch them as they cum. Both breathing heavily as their eyes take me in. The smile on my face is huge as I look at the beauty of them both, the tension in Rafe's face is gone. "I told you I wanted this," I say leaning forward and kissing him. Our lips move together sensually, adding to the sensation when I taste myself on his tongue.

Our lips break with a wet smack, then my eyes get drawn to his length – standing up looking painful. Axel pulls out of him – rolling off the condom and tying the end. His eyes never leave mine as he throws it, I laugh as it goes into the small bin at the side of the nightstand.

"Swish," he says with a laugh, and my eyes nearly bulge out of my head as I see he's still hard even after cuming just now.

"Our turn baby," Rafe growls. Pushing to his feet, he yanks me from my seat. Taking hold of the shirt and ripping the buttons off, the sound of them pinging off surfaces makes me laugh.

He moves me so the backs of my knees are touching the bed, he places a hand on my chest and pushes. I squeal as I fall backwards bouncing on the bed. He turns his attention to Axel, and the smile on his face is so sinful I shudder. I thought I would be running the show, but it looks like he is now. He drops out of view, and Axel's eyes widen. "What's he doing?" I pant with excitement thrumming through me.

"He gets you off while I suck him off," his voice echoes in the room – my brows hit my hairline as I stare at Axel who smirks. "Now get on your knees so we can get to it."

"One second," Axel rumbles, moving to the side of the bed. I hear a drawer open then close.

"Now, we're ready," Axel rumbles dropping to his knees in front of me. My eyes widen as I see the triumphant smirk on his face. I lift a brow in a silent question and his smirk turns into a full-blown smile.

His fingers run through my folds. My head drops back as I groan, his own echoing mine. "Fuck," he growls, as his fingers dip into my core. "You're soaked," he groans again.

My attention gets pulled to the sound of sucking, I jolt up

looking between our bodies as I watch Rafe swallow the length of him, Axel tips his head back moaning again.

"Fucking hell this is hot," I purr, my hand running across the front of his shirt.

"Lie back," he commands, I drop back onto the mattress instantly. His eyes bore into me as I wait, spread open, while I can see his arm moving between my legs.

He bends, taking the bundle of nerves between his teeth as he nips at me. I moan as his fingers pick up the pace. All of us are moaning at the same time, this is *mind* blowing. The sound of something catches my attention a faint buzzing fills the air, and I hear a muffled chuckle from Rafe, as sensation explodes within me. My eyes snap open – taking in the look of lust on Axel's face. The vibrations push into my nerves, and I moan, "Oh fuck, you found my vibe," I pant as the feeling roars through me, and I feel the mother of all orgasms begin to build.

He moans, the sound of gagging fills the room, and I lift my head a little seeing his ass moving. Oh, shit he's fucking Rafe's mouth – the sounds coming from Rafe egg him on as his thrusts pick up the pace. He pushes the vibrator harder into my clit and the orgasm explodes – my scream filling the air, as they both moan loudly.

"Fuck, Majesty," he chuckles as the aftershocks fire off. "Rafe how fucking sexy was that sound?" he asks.

"Mmmm" the sound is his reply as the slurping noises get louder.

"I want one of you to fuck the other, while I ride the other one," I command, my smile is devilish as Rafe's head pops up over the edge of the bed, his eyes are wide as he and Axel look between each other. Rafe scrambles to his feet, as Axel laughs lunging onto the bed – I manage to get out of the way. My laughter fills the air as I watch the pile up of hot bodies.

"So, who's fucking who?" I ask with a lifted brow as I

move to the foot of the bed – pulling off the scrap of fabric left of my shirt since the buttons have disappeared. Axel eyes his handy work with a massive grin on his face. They look to each other contemplating my request, then their eyes meet mine and they both shrug. I tap my index finger against my chin deep in thought when a smile spreads across my face.

"Axel, you mind fucking my boy again?" I ask with a lust filled gaze. "I've not had chance to ride him in a while."

Rafe grins a whole toothed smile as his head bobs in eager agreement, both me and Axel laugh at the response. The sound of a lid popping open has my eyes looking to Axel's hands as he squirts a huge amount of lube onto his palm – his eyes don't leave mine as he takes his length in his hand, pumping his cock between his grasp to make sure he hasn't missed any of it. "Damn that's fucking hot," I mutter as I watch him slide himself forwards, so his feet are hanging off the bed a little.

"Come here you fine piece of ass," he commands, I feel my lust tracking a path down my thighs as Rafe shudders but moves himself on top of him. He moans, his head falling back as he lowers himself onto Axel both of them groan as he fully seats himself to the base.

His back is to Axel's chest as they both eye me panting, I grin as I climb onto the bed on my feet – laughing as I wobble a little from the dip they've made. I swing my leg over so I'm hovering above him reverse cowgirl style. "This, ok?" I ask them both as I see his dick pointing straight up at my core.

They both grunt in agreement, I make sure I've got myself balanced the best I can – I lower myself on his cock, moaning as he stretches me. My walls instantly clamping around him, trying to pull him in further. "Oh fuck," we say in unison. We wobble a bit, but Axel manages to stop us from falling.

"I think Rafe should move. Don't you, Majesty?" Axel rumbles from below me, I throw my head back with a groan as

I place my palms on Rafe's legs to steady myself and make it easier for some leverage for me – but I don't think I'm going to need it.

Rafe thrusts his hips with enough force to lift me onto my toes, I moan as he slides back in with force – His moan echoing mine as he thrusts the best he can so he has both the feel of himself in my core and his arse filled from Axel.

"Fuck, I think I'm going to hell for this," he groans from the bottom of the pile. Rafe's thrusts become more erratic as I try to keep myself steady with the sensations building like a tsunami within me. The sparks start at my centre spreading through my limbs as my moans become half screams, mixed with pants.

"Fuck us both harder," Axel growls, a shudder passes through me at the timber making the bolts of electricity spark faster.

"Fuck, babe, I'm gonna cum," I moan, as I meet him thrust for thrust.

"Play with yourself," they both growl in unison.

I push my weight onto one hand as the other moves down my stomach, towards the bundle of nerves that are throbbing for the release I'm so desperately craving. I circle them, and the bolts buzz harder as I chant "fuck." The feeling is so intense, white dots start dancing in front of my eyes.

"Gorgeous," A voice pulls us out of the moment, my head snaps up. Connecting with Knox's wide eyes. "Fucking hell," he groans looking to the pile up of bodies. I thrust my hips meeting Rafe harder each time, he chuckles in the back of his throat.

"Wow. Fuck that's hot," Deacon's voice joins in, and it's too much – the orgasm builds at a rapid pace.

"Don't just fucking stand there. Either get involved or fuck off," Axel snaps, me and Rafe moan at the same time. My head lifts meeting their lust filled gaze.

"Axel, give me the lube," Rafe purrs, his thrusts becoming shallow. I growl as I try to push him deeper but that arsehole drops his ass onto Axel stopping his thrusts.

"You want her big man?" Deacon chuckles as Knox strides over standing at the foot of the bed, I can see his length standing at attention in his jeans. The tower was the best idea ever, I spent hours researching this on porn sites. But being able to see his reaction is another thing I didn't know I needed until now. He rips his t-shirt over his head, giving me the perfect view of all his tattoos, and bulging muscles. His jeans and underwear drop in an instant, his cock springing free just as quickly.

"Babe, lift up," Rafe commands, I growl not wanting the feeling to disappear not when my orgasm is so close. Knox chuckles darkly as he pulls me up by my hips, and I glare daggers at him as I feel Rafe come out of me. He protests at the loss.

"You ready, gorgeous" Knox growls again as he watches what's going on under my arse.

"Will someone fuck me already," I demand. The orgasm is receding and I don't want that, I want to freefall over the edge of the cliff into the oblivion.

Knox tugs my hips forward – I feel the head pushing against the ring of muscle, I groan as excitement thrums through me. Making me relax enough for the head of Rafe's shaft to penetrate, my groan deepens as he continues pushing into my arse. When he's fully seated and I'm a hot panting mess – the bed dips again. Luckily, we roll a little to the side, I open my eyes – finding Deacon looking down at me with a huge grin, fully naked.

He pushes his thumb between my lips, and I eagerly suck it – my thumb twirling around the pad of the digit. He groans, yanking out his digit, he moves his hips and the tip of his shaft touches my legs. I open my mouth and he thrusts, shallow at first as he pulls my hair off the nape of my neck and pulls my head to the angle he wants.

Rafe's thrust become more punishing as Deacon fucks my mouth with everything he has, his moans mix with ours as I moan around his length – trying my best to suck him at the same time as he thrusts.

"Fuck, Knox, stop fucking about," Axel growls. A snarl responds and then my hips are lifted just a fraction. Then, he thrusts into my centre without warning, his huge size stretching me to an almost painful level. I scream around Deacon, the vibrations making his groan roar out of his throat. Fuck, how are we not falling? Axel is still buried in Rafe, who's now in my arse and Knox has taken up residence in my pussy. Thank fuck for Deacon and him acting as legs to keep us steady.

Knox thrusts into me, at a frantic pace, the feeling of being so full has my head spinning and all my openings that have a length there closing to intensify the feeling. The moans and chants filling the room, egg me on to explode as the orgasm builds like a freight train.

"Play with yourself gorgeous," Knox commands, I drop my chin in answer, forcing Deacon past the gag reflex and I smell his scent at the base of his length.

My hand moves between my legs as I circle the nub, like it's the last thing I will do on this earth. The white spots shimmer to black in my vision as Rafe pounds into my arse and Knox fucks me like a wild animal. The orgasm explodes, my body shaking violently as my vision changes between blackness and then blurry light from the room. I continue to scream as Deacon skull fucks me, his length hitting the back of my throat as Rafe and Knox somehow manage to pick up the pace further. Another orgasm crashes through me and I scream, sweat pouring off me like a river as my body almost convulses with the intensity of feelings inside me at the moment. The blackness rushes in faster as the orgasm reaches its peak once again – my body is alive with the influx of feeling. When it swallows me whole, the last thing I hear are the guys roars as I slip into the oblivion.

CHAPTER SEVENTEEN

My eyes open with the sun streaming through the open curtains. My body feels sore but sated, as I try to wiggle myself into the mattress further. A heavy weight presses in on me, I lift my head a little and find Axel with his thick arm around over my waist, holding me in place. I follow it with my eyes, all the way up to his shoulder – mesmerized by the tattoos filling it. The tribal signs work their way across his shoulder, down onto his pec and up towards his neck. Where there is a bone moth on the front of his neck, it wraps around and I know it connects to a star on the back of his neck, while the rest of the tattoo continues down his back.

A harsh snore fills the air, I chuckle as the sound happens again. I turn my attention from Axel, looking down the length of my body to find Rafe with his head on my stomach, like I'm his own personal pillow. He snores again and I laugh, this time – my stomach jolting his head with the movement.

"Morning, Majesty," the words rumble softly, my core clenches at the sound. I look back to Axel to find him staring at me with a sleepy look on his face. Waking up with any of them like this, makes me sigh with content – but then I never want to leave the bed.

"Morning," I say with a happy sigh as he drops a kiss to my forehead. I look back to Rafe. "I really don't want to wake him."

"I think this is the first unbroken night's sleep he's had in a while," he says with a whisper. Rafe snores again and we both chuckle, as we watch him.

"Stop staring it's creepy," he mutters – lifting his head as he rubs his eyes.

"Morning babe," he says with a smile directed at me. He looks to Axel and my heart just about melts in my chest at the look they share. "Hot stuff."

I bark out a laugh as Axel growls at the side of me, he jumps up from his spot besides me, pushing him with a demonic grin. We both laugh as Rafe yelps as he lands on the floor with a thud.

"Ow," Rafe shouts, peeking over the edge of the bed. The mischief dancing in his eyes has me laughing my ass off as the both throw daggers at each other. It's cute how they both pretend to be annoyed but I know they're happy that they're here.

"Where'd the other two go?" I ask, looking round the room. They aren't here, and I listen to see if I can hear any sounds coming from the bathroom – but there's nothing.

My phone pings on the side, I grab it off the bedside table – finding a message from Knox telling me to hurry my ass up or he will eat the breakfast wraps Deacon is making. I jump out of bed, both the guys look at me confused as I rush into the bathroom. Clicking the button for the shower, I fill the sink while I wait for the shower to warm up. Yeah, I know what you're thinking - why don't they have instant hot water? We did until the guys moved in, as they all have a thing with over cleanliness. It takes a little time to get the water at the right temperature for me. As Axel says, I like to shower in hellfire. I brush my teeth and wash my face as steam fills the room. I smile as I step in, the heat from the water warming my bones. I wash my hair and body in record time, I grab the towel and make my way back into the bedroom.

"Morning sex?" Rafe asks with a heated expression as he and Axel look me up and down like I'm a piece of meat.

"Nope, I've just gotten clean," I say, pulling my underwear on. Next is my uniform. This has to be the fastest I've ever gotten ready for the day, recently. I quickly squeeze the excess water out of my long locks with the towel. Grabbing my brush, I run it through my hair – throwing it on top of my head in a messy bun.

"Oh fuck," a groan has me looking over my shoulder – finding them both wide eyed and almost drooling.

I chuckle, stuffing my feet into my combat boots. I grab the bag off the floor, with a wink over my shoulder to them as they stay on the bed. I chuckle darkly as I get halfway down the hall. "You do know Deacon's made breakfast wraps." I pick up my pace laughing as I hear chaos coming from the room. I get to the top of the stairs, and I hear pounding – I take one last look as both of them thunder down the hall, throwing open their doors and disappearing out of sight.

That was the best day ever. I remember when they found me making one. With confused looks on their face I made one for each of them. They all groaned as they bit into the wrap filled with sausage, bacon, scrambled egg and cheese. Ever since then, whenever they're made, it turns into a war zone for who gets the last one. They seem to forget they can be easily made, I honestly just think it's an excuse to beat the shit out of each other. I make it to the bottom of the stairs, when I hear doors opening – I chuckle as I jog into the kitchen. Both Knox and

Deacon turn to me with smiles on their faces. D has an apron on over the top of his uniform and Knox is already seated at the island, tucking into a wrap.

I sit, grabbing the cup of coffee on my mat – taking a huge mouthful as a crash fills the room. Axel and Rafe fall into the room in a tangle of limbs and grunts as we chuckle. A plate with two wraps is placed in front of me. My mouth starts salivating as the smell invades my nose.

"Morning, babe," Deacon says, dropping a quick kiss onto my lips. I got so lost in him being behind me, and I hear a strange noise. He smirks as I turn my attention back to my food. "Hey!" I snarl noticing I only have one wrap on my plate.

"Ow! What the fuck man?" Rafe screeches, rubbing the back of his head as Knox places the wrap back on my plate with a wink.

"You've both got your own. Leave hers alone," Knox rumbles in warning. He stops them from stealing stuff off my plate when he learnt the lesson the hard way once at dinner. He tried to have a taste of my cheeseburger and I tried to put a fork through his hand. Yep, since then he hasn't tried it again.

"It's going to be chaos there today, beautiful," Knox states, while the deep timber of his voice does weird things to my inside. But right now is not the time and place to use him as my own climbing frame.

"Yeah, well we will deal with it, but how bad do you think the split is?" I throw the question out there, that we've all been thinking since that day in the auditorium – Kylo's presence is becoming an issue.

"I don't know, but we have to be ready. Especially since Axel went on a rampage through the school," Deacon replies with a glower at the man in question.

"Hey," Axel protests. "You helped with the others."

Deacon glares harder making me laugh as both of them are

stuck in a stare off. I see Knox shake his head beside me, while Rafe is tucking into his wrap like a starving man with sauce dripping the edge of his chin.

"Bro, you're worse than an animal," Knox chastises him, Rafe smirks taking a bigger bite this time that has the sauce exploding out the edge of the wrap.

Silence is the only thing now as we all eat our breakfast, and the only sound is my soft moans I make with every bite of food. Deacon pours me another coffee into a to-go cup, while I cock my head in confusion. He taps the watch face on his wrist. *Oh, fuck.* I jump to my feet grabbing the cup and taking the rest of my food with me. We all head out jumping into Knox's truck.

The drive to school was a quick one. Honestly, we could walk there but I think we're all too lazy for that. The campus is bustling this morning, I look to Knox who echoes my concern with a look of his own. There are never this many people out front, "Something's happening," I muse, looking between all the different groups. I climb out of the truck, my feet barely touching the ground and the whispers start – I hike my bag onto my shoulder death glaring some of the wannabes who hiss at me as I walk past.

"Oh looky, the trailer trash is back." Another voice says louder this time. *"I'd have thought they would have thrown away the key with the toxic bitch."* Is another, Knox snarls loudly in warning but the noise continues.

"Do you think when they fuck, she poisons their asses with her toxic cunt."

I spin, gripping the girl by her throat, and she screeches as my hand tightens. "You want to find out sweetie," I say with a savage smile. "My cunt's toxic so that means the rest of me is too," I say chuckling darkly. Her eyes widen as I pucker my lips pulling her closer.

"I'm sorry," she cries in my grasp. "I didn't mean it."

"The only thing toxic is you, you're a washed-out rich bitch who is desperate to get a leg up in this world. Well, sorry to disappoint you but these boys are mine." I state as I toss her ass into the dirt. She looks up at me from her back, tears leaking from the corner of her eyes.

All the guys chuckle behind me as I step over the mouthy bitch and continue on my way to my first lesson. We make it half way across, the guys throwing out commands to the followers and warnings to the arseholes who are shouting shit. The people who have been loyal since the switch of power, take flank behind us as we walk through the corridor – the hushed whispers get louder but that's it.

"I have got to pee," I say to Rafe who's at my side, his eyes narrow a touch, and I can see the anxiety rolling off him in waves. He's on edge. Well, not just him they all are, and I can feel their unease in the air. "You've got classes to get to, and I don't need a babysitter," I growl as they crowd me against the door.

"We're staying," Knox growls, his face set like stone with his "don't argue with me" stance. I look to Deacon who is always the reasonable one in the group, and without fail he blows out a harsh breath, the tension deflating out of him.

"Let's go, you know as well as I do, she will be fine."

I don't give them chance to voice their arguments, I step into the bathroom locking the door on the other side. I've always wondered why there was a lock on this door, but today I'm glad for it. I can hear arguing through the door that's muffled so I know at least a couple of them are pissed about it.

But they need to remember I didn't need a sitter before so I sure as hell won't be having one now. I do my business, and I laugh a few times as I hear the handle rattled and grumbles from someone trying to get in. It's quiet now as I wash my hands. I just turn the tap off when there's a knock on the door.

I chuckle. Toweling off my hands, I throw the towel in the bin. I open the door with an apology on my tongue. But there isn't anyone standing on the other side – what the fuck? I check my phone. *Shit! I'm late.* I take off in the direction of my English language class, my eyes glued to the screen of my phone.

"Bo?" A voice pulls me out of the hole I was in. Standing in front of me is one of the guys I know my guys go to for information. I'm pretty sure he's on the team with Rafe, too.

"What's up?" I ask, turning my attention to him fully. He shuffles from foot-to-foot, his eyes darting everywhere like he's terrified of being seen.

"It was Kylo," he blurts with a tremble to his voice.

"What was Kylo?" I snap losing patience with him, as he keeps looking around.

"He was the one who told the police you did it," he admits quickly, then turns to head off. I grab his arm turning him to face me.

"How do you know?" I demand, tugging on his arm tighter. He stops fighting and turns back to me, his eyes going to something behind me. I see them widen in fear, he grips my arm with his other hand in a painful grasp. I hiss as it throbs through the point of contact, and he drags us back into the corridor I've just come out of.

"He was talking to Jade about it," he says with an anxious expression.

"What do you mean he was talking to Jade?" I demand, my mind racing a mile a minute as puzzle pieces move in my head.

"That's the thing. I was as surprised as you are, so I listened a little longer and heard that she was the one who pushed Tiffany." He says, his eyes pleading with me to believe him.

"I fucking knew it!" My bellow fills the corridor as the final puzzle slots into place in my mind. "Get the guys out of their classes now." He nods his head violently as I stride out of the corridor just as the bell goes. I head toward the library, trying to cut a path through the other students as I do. But there so thickly packed in, I'm getting thrown around like a rag doll.

"You toxic bitch!" A voice screeches, pain radiates through the back of my head as I fall forward – my palms scraping along the stone floor. *"Whore,"* someone bellows, and pain roars through my ribs as I roll onto my side.

My rage explodes as I jump to my feet, finding a group of girls I don't know throwing insults at me. One of them swings again, with a fist this time. I block the move, cracking her in the cheek with a punch of my own. She hits the deck screaming, and I smile savagely at the others.

"Kylo and Jade rule this school," one of the bitches screams at me as her hand snaps out. My cheek stings as she pulls back to slap me again. Her words stoke the rage within me. I fucking knew they were up to something, but this? I should have seen him trying to go for the crown.

A vicious mob surrounds me on all sides as I throw punches at the ones who attacked me. A few of the onlookers have tried to get their own shots in but I've not managed to find out who is the one brave enough to put his hands on me.

Angry shouts fill the air, as the shadows pull back. My head whips up while I still have hold of one of the girl's clothes. My eyes connect with Axel's first. Rage stares back at me as he vibrates with the emotions inside him – that's when I see the others standing there with murderous looks on their faces.

"What the fuck is going on, babe?" Knox asks, as Rafe

pulls the girls' clothing out of my grip. I'm pulled to my feet then, but then the surrounding noise registers. There is silence – it's so quiet you could hear a pin drop. Our friends stand on one side behind my boys, while another group of students face off with them on the other.

My mouth opens and closes like a fish out of water as I pant – my head whips side-to-side, searching.

"Bo?" Deacon voice sounds wary as he steps closer to me, and my eyes lock on the person I was looking for.

I push out of Knox's hold as I charge across the grass towards the carpark. Laughing filters to my ears and my anger builds further. Yells behind me alert the others – eyes widen as I launch off my feet, sailing through the air as a scream fills it.

CHAPTER EIGHTEEN

"I'll fucking kill you," I roar as I land punch after punch. Her face splitting open under the assault. She screams as she wildly tries to defend herself. I jump to my feet grabbing ahold of her top as I do – yanking her onto her feet.

My eyes connect with his, and I pant as I look into his eyes. A slow smirk spreads across his face as I throw another jab hitting her in the nose. "You crazy bitch," someone screams from behind me. But not her. Oh no, the bitch looks me dead in the eye and smirks just like he is.

"I told you I am Queen Bee of this school and you and your little cast-offs can't do anything about it," she says with a snap.

"It's because of the pair of you, I was arrested," I snarl, stepping closer to her. "You want my so-called fucking crown that much, Jade?" I watch as her eyes darken, and she nods her head. "Well come and fucking take it."

I throw my arms out wide, the challenge to her as clear as day. She screams a battle cry launching herself at me wildly. I spin kicking her in the ribs, with enough force to have her stumbling back and I follow the move with another punch. I smile like a man possessed as her nose explodes.

"Fuck her up for me, Bo!" My head snaps to the side to see Wankstein there on crutches with a murderous look aimed at Jade. "Show her the lesson I learnt." I see the guys mouths drop open, and a chuckle builds in my throat. I look to her again and I don't see the hate that used to be there – I nod and wide smile spreads across her face.

"You really think they would want you as Queen Bee when they find out what you did?" I snarl stalking her backwards. She looks behind me, for help.

"Kylo help me," she pleads with him. A growl fills the air as I look over my shoulder, I see the guys blocking his path from us.

"Don't ask him for help," I snarl attacking her again. We fall onto the floor and lose it.

My punches are savage as flesh breaks under the force of impact, screams break out in the crowd. Arms pull at me, trying to pull me off, but I roar my defiance. Managing to push them off so I can keep beating the shit out of her.

"I was a friend to you, and you turned on me," another punch connects. "You turned on me for a guy who wasn't worth shit." My other fist lands. "I stopped you from being raped." My voice is getting louder now. "You let Frost fuck you while his goons forced me to watch."

"Bo!" One of the guys call out to me but I can't stop the verbal vomit. Her face is bloody, her attempts to stop me are becoming sluggish.

"She's going to kill her!" Someone screams as unease fills the air from every person watching.

Arms pull at me as my breathing is chaotic. Buzzing fills my ears as I roar like a wild animal. My vision clears a little to see Axel and Knox staring at me with concern lining their features, two of the guys who were standing on the opposite

146

side pull her to her feet. Holding her up as she lifts her head – they have to hold her upright because I can see she isn't strong enough to do it on her own. Her lips open into a bloody smile as she snarls at me, I manage to push away from the guys getting into her face. I take a deep breath.

"You stood there and watched while your boyfriend raped me." My voice echoes through the area. Gasps fill the air, followed by angry yells and shouts calling me a liar.

"Now what sort of Queen Bee would they think you are, huh?" my eyes stare locked on her.

"You're lying," Kylo shouts, but he doesn't come to her aid. I don't bother turning to face him because he will get his soon enough.

"What the fucks" echo through the crowd as I glare at this bitch I once thought was my friend.

"I always told you, you were mine," echoes around the area and my limbs freeze, my eyes nearly bugging out of my head. Gasps fill the air as the crowd goes nuts. I turn slowly, the guys mirroring my actions.

"Now then little brother, it's time to play with the big boys." I've finally lost my mind. This can't be real but, even so, the voice sends a tremor through me.

"You're dead," Kylo roars at the new comer, a savage smile spreads across his face. Then Kylo is sailing through the air and lands on the floor near our feet in a heap.

"Could a ghost do that?" I look to Knox, his expression mirrors mine.

Frost stands in his spot he's just launched Kylo from, but this doesn't look like him or even my version of him in my dream. He's broader than he was, and he's covered in tattoos from the neck down, full sleeves cover his arms all the way down to the top of his hands. His hair is the same color, but it's shaved closer to his head on the sides, but a little longer on the top. He's wearing mucky ripped jeans with a black tank top, which shows the size of his arms. Knox tucks me into his side protectively as he stares down the person who looks like his old friend, but doesn't. The others crowd in around us, as violent tremors pass through me. My breathing is rapid as I look between the two – confusion clear as I watch Kylo pick himself up of the floor. A savage growl passing his lips as he steps up to the newcomer.

"I sat back and let you have your tantrum brother. But you crossed a line," the ferocity in the voice has my legs shaking, forcing Knox to grip me tighter. I take a deep breath steadying myself. I move out of Knox's grasp, slowly making my way over to the huge force in front of me. I gasp as I get a look at the ice blue eyes that haunt me in my dreams.

"Frost?" I whisper, in shock – my mind has to be playing a trick on me. I lift a shaky hand and gasp as my fingertips meet flesh. "Is it really you?" Hope and terror fill me at this possibly being a lie. He smiles wide, his hand shoots out gripping ahold of the back of my neck - pulling me close. His smell invades my nose, I take quick breathes to pull in more of the scent as a tear escapes the edge of my eye.

"You miss me, Bo-Bo?" He chuckles, showing me with the gleam in his eye, it's him. The look disappears and the cold look is back in place.

"Oh, really Frost? And how did I cross the line, huh?" Kylo snarls spitting at his brother's feet. There is an eerie silence as the brothers face off – Frost pulls me in tighter.

"You crossed the line when you went after her," Frost snarls, the sound filled with so much venom. "No one touches her. If you do, you die."

The crowd backs up, giving a bigger space for the showdown going on as the guys come to stand behind me. Frost drops a kiss onto my forehead and passes me off to Axel. My legs give way under the weight of emotions, and a snarl fills the air.

"This isn't over brother," Kylo spits, backing up but making sure not to take his eyes off his twin.

"Take my advice Kylo, you aren't ready to play with someone like me," the warning is clear from Frost. The crowd shuffles nervously. "But if that's what you really want, then game on." Not one of us takes our eyes off the one who's currently retreating. Some of the students take off behind him and I growl at how quickly they switched sides.

"*Classes are cancelled for the day,*" the words echo as the speakers screeches with an ear splitting sound. *Why the fuck has the dean suddenly cancelled classes?* My eyes lift to the person with his back to me. He turns slowly – I eye him suspiciously and he winks.

"Show's over," Knox bellows, making the remaining students jump with the command. They take off not needing to be told twice. Axel snarls, encouraging them to move faster.

"You never did answer my question, babe," he rumbles with a quirked brow – my eyes run over him shamelessly as I take in my fill. He chuckles again.

"Ow. What the fuck?" He booms, rubbing his cheek, as my palm stings but I pull it back to strike again.

"We buried you," I snarl savagely, punching him in the shoulder. "It fucking destroyed me that day. Then, your brother turns up making us think I was losing my damn mind," I screech, my fists pounding on his chest as I lose it.

"You boys are quiet?" he says over my head as I keep beating his chest, the anger and everything else I'm feeling is all consuming. I growl because he isn't reacting to this – I lean back glaring daggers at him. He looks down at me a slow smile spreading across his face, I lash out catching him on the jaw with enough force to push him back.

"Fuck you for these stupid fucking games you play." I spin on my heels, taking off at speed as I run to the car. Jumping in I hit the lock button as all of them rush over. I throw the car into reverse and peel out of the lot.

CHAPTER NINETEEN

FROST

W e watch as the car peels out of the lot. My nerves are shot as we see the car swerve out into traffic. "What the fuck is she doing?" I bellow, my anxiety going through the roof.

"What the fuck did you expect dude? You show up out the fucking blue without any warning when we all thought you were fucking dead," Deacon snaps at me, taking off across the lot.

"Why would you put her through that?" Rafe snarls, before taking off after Deacon. I watch as both of them, round the gates and head back to the house. Knox hasn't said anything, he's just standing there glaring at me – but that's enough to tell me he's pissed. Axel glares as well with a look of murder shining in his eyes. With a huff, I head over to my car – my eyes going over my shoulder to the other two.

"So, you show up and now you're going to run out on her again. Typical," Knox snarls, his strides eat up the distance as he shoulder checks me with enough force to have me hitting the side of my car. Axel looks me up and down – the anger is clear as he heads off after Knox.

"I'm not running," I blurt the words, both of them turn to face me with lifted brows. "You want a ride back to the house?"

They look to each other, a silent conversation passing between them. Axel makes his way over first. He opens the back door of the truck. "Nah bro I'm not sitting near him," Knox rumbles as he climbs into the back of the truck. I climb in, looking at him through the centre mirror but he doesn't acknowledge me, just stares out of the back window.

"You ready for the shitshow, Frost?" Axel says, with a chuckle, as he clicks in his belt.

"What do you mean?" I ask, confusion must be lining my face as he laughs louder this time and Knox snorts in the back of the car.

"You'll find out," is the only thing he says as he puts the window down and pulls his phone out – his fingers start flying across the screen.

The engine rumbles to life, and I pull out of my spot – then out into the traffic. It doesn't take long for the gates of the house to come into view, something bleeps within the cab. My head whips to Axel who smirks with a weird looking fob in his hand. Once there's enough gap to get through, I put my foot down, gravel kicks up behind us as the front of the house comes into view. Knox's car is parked out front with a few others, both guys blow out a sigh of relief as my nerves start to have a field day inside my veins.

Doors bang as the others jump out and walk straight in, but I find myself sitting in the cab – trying to rein in the war within. With a deep breathe I climb out. My footfalls are slow as I climb the few steps out front. I stand in front of the door, happiness and guilt and everything else building. I never thought I would be standing outside this house again – I knew it would hurt too much.

"You destroy her and then stand on the threshold like a

scared rabbit. I thought you had more balls than that, boy," my head whips around, to find the elderly housekeeper glaring at me with a bag of groceries in her hand. She bends at the hip, placing the bag on the ground – I smile as she straightens, happy to see her. I know she means a lot to her and I'm glad she's still around to support her.

"Hey there Ms. Jea…." I don't have chance to dodge the hit as my already sore cheek roars with pain once again. Her breathing is labored as she pulls her hand back to crack me again. I step back, palms up and she growls like a wild animal.

"I should cut off your damn balls for what you did to that girl," she snarls, jabbing her finger at me. "You have no idea the damage you left behind," My eyes widen at the ferocity of this woman. "Or what me and those poor boys went through since that day, and here you stand freshly risen from the dead like nothing fucking happened."

My mouth opens and clothes as I stare at her, my brain running wild as thoughts of what could of happened over the last few weeks, plays havoc in my mind. *What the fuck went on?*

"I'm sorry," I croak, the apology squeezing the air out of my lungs. "I know I hurt her, but you have to believe me I did what I thought was best," I plead with the woman to believe me.

"I don't give a shit what you did boy, but I will tell you this now. If you've come back to play games with her, I will feed you to some pigs."

I take a step back as she advances. The look on her face tells me the threat isn't bullshit. She pushes past me, heading into the house. With a deep breathe I grab the bag and brave stepping into the house. Nothing hits me as I cross the threshold so that is a bonus – I can hear raised voices coming from the kitchen. I smile at this, glad that the meeting area hasn't changed since I've been here.

"Why the hell are you blaming us for this," Knox's voice booms, his words bouncing of the walls.

"You all must have known what he was up too," the emotion in her voice has me cringing. "His death fucking broke me, Knox." My heart crumbles at the confession, the emotion clear in her voice as I hear a hiccup. "Don't you get it? I can't do this shit again."

"Why the fuck would he come back now?" Rafe growls, the sound of legs scraping across the floor, has me moving to the side of the wall so I can sneak a look into the room.

"I know you're out there boy, you best get your ass in here and sort out the chaos you've caused," Ms. Jeanette growls, I inhale deeply – my grip tightens on the grocery bag as I step into the madness.

"You left this on the step," I say, with a pointed look to her. My eyes narrow as she smirks at me. I notice her shoulder move and I see her rubbing circles on Bo's back to soothe her. Tears stream down her face, and the sight guts me – it feels like someone has taken a blunt knife and stabbed it through my heart.

"What the fuck, Frost?" Deacon bellows. "Will you fucking tell us what the fuck is going on?" A glass crashes against the wall at the side of my head, and I can't help but smile at the hostility from him – he's always been so quiet and only ever lost his shit when needed, but this new version of him is amazing.

"Who did we bury?" her words sound hollow as she stares at me with tears in her eyes from across the room.

"My dad," I say with no remorse – all their heads snap back at the confession. Do I feel anything for him being dead? Do I fuck – it took me a while to see how he used me as his puppet, but, as I said to my long-lost twin, he made the mistake of going after her.

"You're saying I lost it over your fucking dad being lowered into the ground?" she snarls pulling herself to her feet. If looks could kill, I would be in the family plot – she looks me up and down. Her anger is so potent, it rolls off her in waves – chairs scrape as the guys all move away from the island, even Ms. Jeanette moves back.

Another glass smashes against the wall at the side of my head, and I have to duck to stop the shards from hitting my face. I look to see she's vibrating with the emotions within, and this time she grabs a bottle and raises it. "If he was dead, why didn't you come back when it was over?"

I eye the guys as their attention turns to me, and nervousness plays havoc in my system. "Because it was better for everyone if I left," the words are hollow as I admit the reason why.

The bottle hits the floor by my feet, I jump back – watching as the shards glitter like tiny diamonds. "Better for who?" she asks with a snap of her voice, "You?"

"Don't play that shit, Bo. You know as well as I do that I repeatedly hurt you," I snap losing my patience. "I knew they would look after you, so I left. I knew they could be what you needed, and I wanted you to be happy," I say with an exasperated sigh.

"And you thought that didn't include you?" Deacon says, his eyes wide as he watches me. I feel like my heart's trying to beat out of my chest.

"You know the stuff I did to her willingly. Yeah, he used me as his puppet, but I'm not going to lie about that time I enjoyed what I put her through," I admit, my words even so nobody can question my feelings on this.

"Why do you look so different?" Ms. Jeanette asks, her eyes

look me over as her eyebrows drop into a frown. "I'm sorry, boy, but you look like you, but not."

I bark out a laugh. You can't help but not like the woman – she does grow on you eventually. The way she questions everything and asks the questions that most people are afraid to ask. "This is my way of feeling."

"What do you mean?" Bo asks. I watch with suspicion as she rounds the island, coming to stand in front of me. The scent of the vanilla body wash she uses invades my senses and I groan. The urge to pull her into me is strong. I want to bury myself in the feel of her, but I know I can't do that.

"The changes you see, and some you can't, were my way of feeling the pain I put you through before," I admit, taking a deep breathe. "And it was payback for what you went through at the funeral."

"What do you mean?" her lower lip trembles, the emotion clear on her face. I place my hands on her hips pulling her closer – I lift my left hand, the tips of my fingers brushing up the front of her uniform as I grip a hold of her throat, my thumb pushing up on her chin to lift her head, so her eyes meet mine.

"I had to see you one last time before I left. So, I stopped by the funeral on my way out of town. I just couldn't leave without seeing you, but then seeing the pain you went through, I knew it was the best decision I could make," I confess." You don't see it, Bo, but I love you in my own twisted way and I couldn't put you through anymore hurt."

"Don't you think that was my choice to make?" She hiccups as tears escape the corners of her eyes, and guilt fills me at the pain she's feeling now. I close my eyes, pressing my forehead to hers – I inhale as much of her scent as I can. A phantom knife twists in my stomach as guilt fills me.

"This is the best thing for you. I need to get back. Kylo's going to try to come at you full force now and I can't allow that." I growl, the thought of what he will try and do now drives me to insanity. I drop a kiss on her forehead, taking the time to inhale as much of her as I can to remember. I release my hold quickly as I turn on my heels and head towards the door.

"You're leaving me again," her words are broken, I pick up the pace trying to put as much distance as I can between us. I shouldn't have come back as soon as I heard what was going on, but he was becoming braver so I had to show my face. I've managed to stop him from getting too close to her since he came back but this? I couldn't sit back and leave it to the others.

"Frost, don't you fucking walk away from this," she roars, she grips my arm with a strong grip – stopping me in my tracks as she spins me to face her.

"Don't you get it? I love you," I bellow. The thin wire I was on finally snapping. "I love you so fucking much, and I don't want to hurt you because of how fucked I am."

She stands there wide eyed, chest rising and falling rapidly as we stare at one another. She doesn't say anything for a long time, but her eyes never leave mine. She steps closer. I inhale harshly as her eyes look me over slowly. Her head tips up to meet my eyes but there are a wildfire of emotions filtering in her eyes that I can't see to work out what's going on in her head. She launches off her feet, her lips crashing down on mine. I groan at the feel of her up against me, I groan as our lips devour each other. I feel her legs circle my hips as she tightens the hold she has on my neck.

The moan that leaves her has my dick jumping to a painful level. I was already semi-hard earlier in the kitchen knowing she's so close with that damn skirt on has me biting into her bottom lip. "Fuck baby, I've missed you," I groan as she nips at my neck. I wrap my hand in her hair pulling her head back sharply. Her replying whimper has a savage sound coming out between my teeth as I crash my lips down on hers once more. I blindly take off with determined strides as our tongues battle for dominance. The door creaks behind me, Bo doesn't even notice as she claws at my neck. I slam her back against the wall at the side of the door – breaking the kiss with a wet smack. She pulls back, breathing frantic. Her eyes widen when she realizes we're in her room. I smile wide as I wrap my hand around her throat again, squeezing just a little and she purrs.

I growl, my other hand going between us as I pull her underwear to the side – my thumb sliding between her folds, she throws her head back with a moan as I feel how wet she is for me. I brush the nerves with the pad of my thumb, her body jolting from the feeling. As I thrust two fingers into her, she moans louder. I run my tongue across my lip, her eyes meet mine and widen. I chuckle as her eyes track the movement.

"Is that?" she asks between pants as I continue to finger fuck her. I smile, her eyes almost roll in her head – as she cries and chants "oh fuck" as I feel her walls clamp down on my fingers. I pull my fingers out, she cries out at being empty. Her eyes snap to mine. As I rip the shirt open, her mouth drops open with a gasp.

I reach behind her, my hand undoing the clasp of her bra in one movement. I watch as it falls to her elbows, my mouth waters as her pink nipples call me. I suck one into my mouth, nipping the bud with my teeth as I squeeze the other with my free hand. Her moans spur me on as I switch moving to the other and start the assault on that one with my tongue and teeth.

"You're wearing way too many clothes for this," she snaps, I chuckle darkly with her nipple in my mouth. I drop it with a pop, licking my lips as I grip her neck again. I pull her into my chest I spin striding across the room. Dropping her ass on the bed she gasps as I pull the tank top over my head.

"How far do they go?" she asks her eyes tracing over my chest and abdomen.

"There is only the bottom of my feet, face and head clear," I growl, gripping her around the ankles – I drag her to the edge of the bed, bending at the waist I kiss her again until she moans against my mouth. The buckle on my belt clicks together as I unbuckle it, my eyes on hers. I quirk a brow in a silent command, and she giggles – making me smile as she loses the scraps of her shirt. I unbutton my jeans, so they drop lower on my hips, she quirks a brow licking her lips when she realizes I wasn't lying about my tattoos.

My eyes devour her body as I look her over, the scar on her side is something of beauty. I know she plays off like it doesn't bother her, but I know deep down it must. I know the damage was caused by her being impaled on something in the accident. The rescue services found her, her heartbeat faint but enough for them to save her.

"Stop staring at it and fuck me already," she growls, I smirk at the sass – I lean over her, hands either side of her head.

"I'll look at it all I want," I growl as my fingers trace the scar. "It tells me the story of how much of a warrior you are."

Her eyes widen as I smile, her cheeks flush pink with embarrassment. I chuckle darkly as she hides her face. I tug her closer to the edge of the bed, and lifting her hips I slam into her in one powerful thrust. She screams, the sound echoes off the wall – it spurs me on as I pull out and thrust into her again. My pace quickens with each movement, she thrashes her head as I fuck her like the sky is falling.

"Oh. My. Fucking. God," she chants as the sound of flesh hitting flesh. "What the fuck is that I'm feeling?" I chuckle, slowing my hips so my thrusts are shallow, and allowing her to feel the whole of the sensations going on. Her walls squeeze my dick like it's a vice around me, making my head roll back and pulling a guttural moan out of me.

"Oh, fuck, Bo! Bo, you're so fucking tight."

"Oh my god, Frost," her head rolls again, her walls clamping down on me even harder and I have to fight back my orgasm, not wanting to blow my load to soon.

"You remember when I said I wanted to put myself through as much pain as possible?" she nods her head, but only barely as her moans, mix with her pants. Sweat gathers on her brow, as I feel her orgasm start to reach its peak. I stop my thrusts so I'm fully seated to the hilt.

"Yeah, well one of the things, baby, was I got a full Jacob's ladder," I grin as her eyes widen, I roll my hips to intensify the feeling, and the sound she releases is almost feral.

"Do I need to kill a bitch?" she asks with a serious look on her face, and my cock pulses at the murderous look on her face. *Fuck my life*. She's just as fierce as she was when I first saw her.

"I fucked up before." I thrust harder, so she moans – her flesh pebbling with goosebumps. "I know that, now," I growl as I thrust harder. "But," I pant as my hips start to pound into her – like they're attached to a puppet's strings and she's the puppet master. "There is only you."

She screams as I fuck her, my hips pounding into her so hard, she starts to move up the bed, I have to hold her hips to anchor her in the spot. The bed slams against the wall – her moans grow louder. As I feel the sparks start building her walls tighten down like they're about to go into a spasm. My balls tighten as sweat runs between my shoulder blades. She screams, and I explode – my cock pulsating deep as I roar my release, her walls milking me for everything they can. I fall forward, still connected to her – our foreheads touching as I pump slowly in and out. Driving her through her aftershocks as she trembles beneath me. I pull out, my eyes going straight to her pussy as I watch our cum starting to leak out. My eyes connect with hers as I scoop the juices up that have escaped and push it back in burying my fingers as deep as I can get them.

"That's better," I smirk as she stares at me in post-orgasmic bliss. I pull out my fingers, and they shimmer with evidence of what we've just done. Without breaking eye contact, I suck my fingers clean – chuckling as I roll onto my side. I pull her up further on the bed with me, so we're laying on the pillows. Her eyes trace the lines of my face working their way down my body. Her eyes snap up to mine and then back to my junk as all the metal in it shines.

"You weren't joking?" she says looking back to my length. "Is that a tattoo?" she asks with a whisper.

"You asking if my dick is tattooed?" I chuckle. "Yeah, Bo-Bo, it is." She winces at my words, and I bark out a laugh at the horror that replaces the look of shock. She moves closer, tucking herself into my neck so her head is resting on my shoulder, as her arm comes across and circles my chest.

"Shit, sorry, you two," Rafe says with a sheepish look. "Nice metal bro," he jokes. I smirk at him. His eyes find Bo curled up at my side. "I've had a call, my dad wants to see me," he says.

"You want me to come with you?" she asks, pulling out of my hold.

"No, it's all good gorgeous. Plus, I think you've got some catching up to do," he says with a smirk. "Be good kids," he chuckles as he shuts the door. We chuckle as we hear him laughing his ass off as he heads downstairs – making sure he tells the others I've got my dick pierced.

Bo yawns at the side of me, I smile as she snuggles back into my neck. "I probably won't be here when you wake up," I say, her head whips up from her position to glare at me. My lids

161

become heavier as sleep takes me willingly this time around and I know it's down to having her in my arms.

"I've got some explaining to do on why I'm back from the dead," I say with a yawn, I feel her nod into the crook of my neck, her breathing becomes heavier, and I feel her breath against my skin which lulls me. My eyes close as my breathing deepens, the call of sleep too strong now as a contented sigh leaves me while I drift off with my girl in my arms.

CHAPTER TWENTY

BO

"*What is that smell?*" *I cough as I look around the room finding myself standing next to my library door, which is on the other side of my bedroom. Smoke comes from under the door, forcing me to cover my mouth, coughing as it gets into my lungs. I look to the bed and Frost isn't there. I rush over to my wardrobe. Pulling out a t-shirt, I cover my mouth to try and stop myself from inhaling the smoke. Cautiously, I walk over to the door, touching the handle with the back of my hand. I throw the door open, the smoke engulfing me as I step out into the hallway. This is a dream. "Bo, wake up!" I command myself as my eyes look down the hallway which goes to the other side of the house. I jump back as flames lick the walls, and it eats its way through the house.*

"It's just a fucking dream! Wake up!" I scream out loud trying to break myself out of this nightmare. My eyes stream - the shirt not blocking the smoke. I start hacking, and my throat feeling like it's closing in on itself trying to choke me. I feel around trying to make my way through the house, but my vision is impaired, from how thick the blackness is.

"Bo," My head whips around trying to find Axel, but I

can't, and I begin to feel light-headed, and my muscles become weaker as I stumble forward. I open my mouth to call out to him, but nothing comes out but a croak, then another round of coughing.

"Majesty, wake up. C'mon, I need you to open them pretty eyes for me." What does he mean open my eyes? I'm trying to get out of the dream, it's not real – I'm dreaming. I fall to my knees, curling into a ball as my body feels like it's seconds away from giving up on me.

"Bo! Open your fucking eyes!"

My eyes open a fraction but tears stream down my face as I cough. My chest feels like it's burning. I can see figures dancing like black dots in front of me, and someone scoops me up marital style, but I can't see. The blackness is so thick. "What's happening," I croak between coughs.

"Oh, thank fuck," Axel growls. My eyes shoot open seeing he's the one carrying me as he runs down the stairs. A roaring sound comes from behind him just as he gets to the front door. I see the backside of the house in flames. The fire is devouring everything in its path.

"Axel, Ms. Jeanette's in there," I scream as I fight to get free. He puts me down on the grass. Deacon and Knox sit beside me coughing, their eyes bloodshot and streaming. I scramble to my feet, and my body sways as I take a step forward. "We've got to get her out," I scream as strong arms circle me.

"Majesty, she's safe," he says tightening his hold on me. My head snaps to the side and I can see the worry on his face. I start coughing again, my chest feeling like a boulder is crushing it under its weight. "She told us she was going to the trader's market last night. She's safe."

"Where's Rafe?" I bark. Between the pain in my throat and my chest, it comes out hoarse.

"He's with his dad remember?" Knox says, his concern-filled gaze on me.

Sirens wail as emergency services comes barreling down the driveway. The fire truck's lights fill the air with their bright colours just as two ambulances pull up. The EMTs rush over, the guys refusing to be examined until they've looked at me. The woman is trying to talk to me, but I can't tear my eyes away from the sight in front of me. The flames are roaring through the windows on the front of the house as the firefighters try to get it under control. A sob escapes me as I watch my home burn. The female EMT manages to get me in the back of the ambulance with help from Knox. I see her moving around me, but I can't take my eyes off the scene. It's as if something is holding my head in place – forcing me to watch. Yells fill the air as a huge groan fills the night sky, and the house sways to the right. Firefighters rush out the front door, two of them have something between them, and they make it out just as the house collapses behind them.

"Knox, what is that?" I ask. The words are muffled through the oxygen mask on my face – the guys look between us and the firemen. The color drains from Deacon's face as they drag closer whatever they hauled out of the house. My eyes widen as I work out the shape of it. I rip the mask off over my head, taking off in the direction of the men. My screams fill the air. All the guys grab at me as I run across the grounds, and police officers jump in my way to block my path, but I manage to avoid them too. My knees give way, as the smell of charred flesh assaults my nose. The body lying on the ground is unrecognizable. The scream that tears from my throat is haunting.

"Who is it?" I scream as one of the officers covers the body from view. My heart turns to dust in my chest as I scream into the air. Arms surround me from all directions.

"Has anyone spoke to Rafe or Ms. Jeanette?" I plead with the guys. My head lifts to meet the horrified faces, all three of them are pale white. They shake their heads, and my legs shake as my soul shatters into a million pieces.

"Excuse me, Miss?" A voice has me looking around for the owner to find an officer standing beside Knox, who looks like he's about to throw up.

"We have some questions for you," I nod my head, looking to Deacon for support. "Alone. My colleagues have questions for you boys, too." They begin to protest, I shake my head following the officer away from them, my limbs feeling heavy as a numbness settles over me.

Shivers rack my body as the cold finally manages to penetrate through the numb shield I have surrounded myself with while the officer finishes his questioning. He did huff every now and then as I answered his interrogation robotically. The way he asked them and tried to goad me for an answer really started to piss me off, but then every time my anger built, I remembered the body on the ground. They took the body to find out who it was. They're referring to the body as a John Doe, at the moment. The officer did say some people would be in touch when the investigation was over to tell us how the fire started, but, honestly, he used unfamiliar words that went straight over my head. My concern, at the moment, is finding out who the body belongs to. Rafe isn't answering his phone, neither is Frost, and Ms. Jeanette's is going to voicemail.

"Miss, do you have somewhere to stay tonight?" The officer's voice pulls me out of the pit of my own mind, and my hand falls away from my mouth. A stinging sensation spreads up my hand from my fingers. I look down to see I've chewed my nails down to the bed as little drops of blood bead on the tips of two of them.

"Um," I reply with a desolate tone, my eyes stare at the wet ground – I dig my toes into the ground. Watching as the mud buries my toes like its quicksand, I grind a little harder as my teeth bite into my bottom lip and I feel the tears pooling in the corner of my eyes.

"Yeah, we do officer, she has a cabin which was left to her, too," Deacon says with a deep timber. The officer mutters something so fast I don't hear it. He pulls me into his side just as another shiver washes over me, and two more shadows press in on ours.

They lead me to Knox's Jeep since it's the only one that isn't covered in debris and ashes from the fire, I don't know how it's possible but my car and Axel's truck look like they were parked next to a volcano when it erupted. I did hear some of the firefighters say that it was bad as some of the trees caught alight, too, from the blaze. A sob builds and I double over, the guilt heavy as I think how lucky we are to be standing here, but also not knowing who they pulled out.

Axel hauls me into the backseat and climbs in after me, forcing me to slide over so he can get in – I hear the front doors open and close. My thumb comes to my mouth, I start chewing on the skin around the nail, as I stare out of the window. Axel tries to pull me onto his lap, but I stop him with a shake of my head – I don't want comfort, now. I need to know who did this so I can figure out who I need to get my revenge on for whoever the body belongs to. When I find out who is responsible for this, I will raze the earth to ground to get my vengeance. Growls fill the car, and my head whips up as my eyes connect with three sets of eyes all staring at me with frightening expressions.

"They will pay, Majesty. Make no mistake about that," Axel rumbles, the other two nod in agreement. With a sharp nod, I turn my attention back out of the window – the numbness is still there but a layer of it has pulled back allowing rage to show its face.

The rumble of the engine quietens the car, as I watch the streets turn quiet with only the occasional person milling around, which is fine after the chaos outside of the gates. People lined the street with false concern, and I know they were trying to get the lowdown on what happened. However, they soon moved out of the way when it looked like Knox was prepared to run someone over, if need be. The streets turn from close knit buildings to a layout where there is more distance between them. Then, it turns to forest roads, the trees flying past. The car rumbles as it picks up speed with Knox taking the corners faster than he should - but honestly, I don't give a shit at the moment.

The car takes a right and the smooth road turns into a bumpy track, jostling us all over the place. The sunrise starts to break through the trees, as the cabin comes into view. Knox slams to a stop as the brakes protest. I jump out, striding to the door – my legs eating up the ground. The twigs and stuff covering the floor bite into the soles of my feet, but I don't feel a thing, as I climb the stairs throwing the door open. There's no need to lock the door here because no one ever comes this far out. Well, more so because they would much rather travel to some rich bastard's area where they can be served cocktails by the pool.

The door creaks a little as it swings open, revealing the open-plan kitchen. The huge staircase is off to the side near the open fireplace. Trees surround us all around and the road is far enough away that we can't hear any traffic that happens to drive down the road – but, then again, it's very rare we see any other vehicles. I walk mechanically through the house; I make it to the front of the fridge, and grab a glass off the shelf. I place it in the automatic water dispenser, and the clink of ice dropping into it sounds like a tinkling melody as the water fills up the glass.

"Why don't you let me make you a warm drink and some food?" Knox asks from behind me. I grab the glass and bringing it to my lips I take a huge gulp – the feel of it is like shards going down my parched throat. I shake my head, not bothering to answer as the willingness to talk has disappeared.

"Bo, why don't you go up to the bedroom to rest?" Deacon asks. I turn to face them and see all their eyes on me. We all must have the same expression on our faces. The guys have lines of ash on their faces, too.

"I don't want to sleep," I growl, the glass shaking in my hand with enough force to make some of it slosh over the side. All of them look deflated as I stare off into space. My body is frozen, but I can't bring myself to go up and get changed.

"Fuck this! I need something stronger," I growl, placing the glass on the island with a clink, because it slipped through my hand because of the condensation on the side of it. I walk through to the living room. Opening the liquor cabinet in the bookcase, I grab the bottle of whiskey and a glass. I watch intently as I fill it up almost to the rim. I place the bottle down with a bang, and tipping my head back I swallow half of it in one go. The burn down my throat is a welcome feeling as I gulp down the rest of the glass. I wipe the corner of my mouth with the back of my hand. I fill the glass again, and the guys glare at me as I make it a pattern. It doesn't take long for the effects to kick in as my body feels lighter.

"Shots," I shout turning my attention to the guys. They eye me suspiciously, but I shrug as I fill my glass up again. I tip it in their direction, and I watch as they move into the living area.

Knox comes over, looking down at me from his towering height. "C'mon, Knoxy, I think we deserve to have a drink after the shitshow of this morning, don't you?"

"Bo, I think you need to get some sleep," he rumbles against my ear. "Why don't we go up to bed?"

"How about no?" I giggle as my mind finishes the sentence from the viral videos on social media. I double over with laughter from the look on his face, and even Axel sniggers. Knox looks at me like a disappointed parent would a misbehaving child. "Put a cork in it, Knox. Either get drunk with me or piss off," I huff - draining the contents and filling the glass.

Axel comes over grabbing a bottle of vodka out of the cabinet, not bothering to get a glass as he flicks the cap off with a precision. I laugh harder as it pings across the floor - Deacon's eyes following it as it slides to a stop somewhere in the kitchen.

"Are either of you going to help me with her or not," Knox growls at the other two. Axel's currently chugging down the bottle of vodka like it's water. Deacon shrugs, walking over to me with a smile on his face. He grabs the bottle of bourbon with two glasses. He fills them both and hands one of them to Knox.

"May as well join them, dude," he says, with a shrug as he knocks his drink back. I smile wide as Knox does the same, their glasses filling as soon as the contents have gone. I sway a little bit - the floating feeling you get when the alcohol is deciding to kick your arse or not is in full effect. I look at the bottle and frown as I see there's only half of it left, but fuck it – I grab the other one out of the cabinet. I walk over to the huge sectional, dropping onto my arse. My feet scream in relief, and I look at them – confused as I see the grime and blood mottled into the flooring. Huh! That's going to hurt in the morning.

I nestle myself into the massive mound of cushions, drinking from the bottle. Axel comes and sits on my left and Deacon on my right. Both drink their drinks as Knox takes a seat on the massive oak coffee table in front of me. The others drink with gusto, and his eyes narrow on me and I smile, lifting my finger in the air. He downs his drink and then fills it again. After fifteen minutes, all of us are giggling like a set of idiots with the alcohol splashing all over the place as Axel tries to twerk on the sofa and falls over the back. I spray my mouthful of drink everywhere as I nearly fall of the sofa laughing. Knox is howling and Deacon looks like he's about to pass out, due to lack of oxygen.

"What the hell is going on here?" a voice booms. I peek over the top of the sofa, busting out laughing as Knox and Deacon lose their shit while Axel gives Frost a thumbs up from the floor.

CHAPTER TWENTY-ONE

"I got all your messages," he fumes, coming over to the sectional. He has to step over Axel to stand behind me, and his ice blue eyes glint in the sunlight. *Wow, he really does have pretty eyes.* "Will someone explain to me what the hell is going on?" he barks.

We all lose it laughing our arse's off like this shit is the funniest thing we have ever heard. Knox falls off the table with an almighty crash. My howls fill the air, I tip up the bottle, but nothing hits my tongue – I squint through the glass, my eyes narrowing as I realize it's empty. I grab for the bottle sitting between my legs, but there's nothing but air. A bark of laughter has me looking over the back of the sofa to see Axel laying on the floor with the empty whiskey bottle wiggling in my face.

"You drank my liquor?" I snarl, as the other two start laughing again. "Frost, be a doll will you, and grab us another bottle from the back of the kitchen?" I bat my eyes, with a wide smile – his eyes narrow a touch, but then he laughs.

"Fine, but just because some of us look like heathens doesn't mean we have to act like ones too," he says, his voice echoing from the other room. I can hear the faint clink of bottles, then a tinkling fills the sound. He comes back in with four glasses filled with whiskey, and he passes them off to each of us. I smile and empty the contents down my throat. He comes back into the room with a drink of his own – his eyes going to each of us.

"Majesty, you know what this means?" Axel asks, his words slurred.

"What are you talking about, you idiot?" Deacon gripes as he finishes his glass.

"Frost isn't the body from the fire so that leaves two others."

Pain roars to life in the back of my throat, like it's suffocating me. My chin drops to my chest as the guilt flares back to life with vengeance. The whole room has quieted as we all get hit with whatever emotions, at the moment. They're safe. They have to be – I know what Rafe's like when something happens with his dad. He loses track of time because his mother hen instincts kick in and the nurses normally have to throw his ass out. Ms. Jeanette always spends ages at the market, she either meets Angie there and they have coffee and buy the stuff they need, or she ends up helping someone with something.

"You ok Bo-Bo?" Frost asks, a look of concern on his face. I look out the window – not knowing how to answer him.

I stumble over the back of the sofa, only just managing to miss falling on Axel as my legs buckle beneath me. I'm able to steady myself, but my legs shake as I walk out and up the stairs – my hand gripping tightly to the rail making sure my ass doesn't roll down the stairs. I breathe a sigh of relief as my foot hits the top step. I head down the hallway – the bathroom is located in halfway down the hallway. I do my business since my bladder felt like a water balloon downstairs. I wash my hands, staring at my reflection in the mirror. My eyes are still blood shot and ash lines my face. My sleep shorts and Deacon's oversized white t-shirt is mottled grey because of the smoke. A buzzing sound builds in my head, making the room spin – I cup water in my hands, splashing it on my face to try and relieve the effects of the alcohol. The room spins, forcing me to death grip the vanity to stop myself from falling. *Woah!* Everything tilts, my legs buckle, and I drop to my knees. I pull myself up, and my veins purr with the alcohol. *Fuck! I think I've had way too much to drink.* I stumble down the hall with the room swaying every chance it gets – I somehow make it down the stairs, but my head feels foggy. My limbs are feeling heavier.

"Frost?" I call out to him as I fall sideways, and my body crashes to the floor – I hiss, as my body screams at the impact from the wooden floor. My vision darkens as I lay here panting, as nausea washes over me, and I see a shadow in front of my face.

"Babe, you ok?" his voice rumbles from the shadow above me. I open my mouth to reply but I can't. My limbs feel heavy. I try to lift my head, but my limbs don't want to cooperate.

Something brushes against me, well that's what it feels like, anyway – I want to yell out as fear takes over. I've been totally shitfaced before but never like this. There's a huge crash and muffled voices – I try to lift my head again, but it feels like something is tied around my neck keeping me in place. Another crash rings out around the room, with yelling and a commotion going on. The darkness rushes in from the corners of my vision. The voices get further away and then the void swallows me.

CHAPTER TWENTY-TWO

A harsh thumping sound has a snarl escaping. *Who the fuck is banging on the door at this time?* The sound becomes louder, and realization dawns on me as I peel my eyes open – I can hear my headache. *What the actual fuck?* My vision is blurry at first, nothing stands out – the fog clears. I'm sitting in a dark room with a small window high up that lets in some moonlight that shines into the corner of the room. I sit up further when a clink catches my attention, then pain roars to life in my wrists.

"Majesty?" my head whips to the side, my eyes widening as I see the guys all chained to what looks like metal columns. I look around, taking in everything. We're in some sort of warehouse thing, but the place looks to have been empty for years. *What the hell happened?* Memories flash to the front of my mind – the fire, us getting drunk at the cabin. Frost coming back which was a relief but then everything went black.

"What the fuck happened?" I ask my voice soft, my gut telling me I can't lose my shit like I want to. "We were having a blast, all things considered, then everything went black not long after Frost came back."

"It wasn't me babe," his tone has a shudder washing over me. My brain pulls the memory to the front and almost freezes it in my mind like a photograph – I scrutinize everything.

"What do you mean it wasn't you?" I growl, with annoyance and pain, as my shoulders start to ache from being pulled behind me. How long have we been here?"

"Frost you need to tell her," Knox growls, his voice slightly slurred – so the words come out, but sound a little jumbled.

A harsh breath blows out, then I hear the clinks of metal again. Someone must be moving, the sound of denim on the floor can be heard. "It was Kylo."

"No. There's no fucking way that could have been him. We would have known it wasn't you," I bark, the sound harsh in the building. My words echo from the volume.

"It was. I walked in as he was leaning over you on the island. I don't know what he was planning but I got there just in time," he admits his voice drawn out – like he's replaying the scene in his mind. "I heard him, as I walked in, saying to you that he wanted to find out why we're so obsessed with you. I reacted on instinct, punching him in the head, you fell. Then a group of people burst through the door with ski masks on. Something hit the side of my neck and the next thing I know I wake up here, seeing you all here - chained, too."

"Is Rafe here?" I ask, horror filling me that there's a chance they managed to grab him too.

"No, gorgeous, he isn't," Knox answers, my chest deflates a little with relief that he isn't – but then that leaves the question, *where the fuck is he*?

"Glad to see all our guests are now awake," a voice booms through the area, I squint into the darkness – but I can't make anyone out. "How are you all doing with the side effects from the drugs you were given?"

"Who the fuck are you?" Frost bellows. The voice chuckles

darkly and a sense of dread fills me. *Who the fuck is this*? I replay the voice in my head, trying to work out if I've heard it before.

"Oh, Bo, what a cute concentration face you have," the voice chuckles again. "You don't know me girl, but I definitely know you." The sound of shoes clicking against concrete surrounds us, then another set join in with the first. That means there's two people here, another set echoes the sound making its own tune. Three, there's three people – *we're screwed.*

"Good to see you again, Miss Walker," another voice says. My blood turns to ice, and a feral snarl passes my lips as I tug on my bindings.

"Novack, you motherfucker," I snarl. I stumble to get up. The aftereffects of the drugs still have me feeling weak, but I manage to get onto my knees. When something clicks and the area is filled with blazing lights, my eyes close. I breathe through my nose trying to centre myself. When I open them again, the light doesn't blind me, and I can see Novack standing behind a man and woman.

"Novack, you're dead, you bastard," Frost snarls. "I'll fucking gut you, you traitorous asshole."

"Fuck you, Frost. You're the reason your father fucked me over. If you had of done what he tasked you to do and not get attached to this little bitch, I would be sitting on a beach somewhere," he roars, I see his chest rising and falling rapidly, but most of my attention is on the other people here. The man looks familiar but I'm certain I've never seen him before.

"When you killed your father for a bit of trailer-trash pussy, the deal we made fell through. So, I took it upon myself to make sure I get what I was owed." Novack fumes, stepping closer to Frost.

"Enough," the other man roars, quieting the room. "We don't have time for this shit, we need to get this train moving."

"I should have known you would try something," Axel growls, his voice thick with venom. "You should have just come after me, Adam. I was the one who tore your rapist son to pieces."

What the? My eyes hit my hairline as I watch as his calm demeanor changes instantly. His face is bright red in a matter of seconds and his lips pucker. The woman at his side pales. *Oh fuck.* Now, I know why he looks so familiar – I look him over, and the resemblance is uncanny. This man is Titan's father. He looks like an older version of him - the only difference is he's a little smaller than his son was and he has grey hairs that pepper the side of his head.

He roars, and the sound bounces off the walls – the noise is like a wild animal. He launches at Axel, his fist connecting with his face. We all yell as he throws punch after punch – the guys tug at their restraints trying to break free. Axel takes the blows with a savage bloody smile. My screams for the man to stop fill the air. His head whips around his gaze settling on me.

"Stop it," I yell again. "What do you want from us?" I kneel, panting, as I watch emotions play across his face. Axel is still in his grasp – his head rolling to the side as blood covers his face and down his shirt. The other two call out to him but he doesn't respond, and my gut twists at him getting beaten. I know this fucker only did it now because he knows he wouldn't stand a chance against him if he wasn't chained. *Bastard!*

"Don't touch him again," I snarl tugging on my chains as he turns his attention back to the one piece of my soul. He pulls his fist back, murder clear in his eyes.

"I'll do anything, just leave him the fuck alone!" I snap. His head whips around to me – his gaze running over me as if he's scrutinizing me. I lift my chin, looking up at him, and he smiles a demonic smile as he drops Axel onto the floor. Pulling himself to his full height he runs his palms down the lapels on the front of his suit jacket. Blood smears the white shirt beneath.

"I won't touch any of them," he says with a triumphant smirk. "All you have to do is sign everything over to us."

"Bo don't do it, babe," Frost bellows. Knox echoing his agreement with a snarl. My eyes flick between the man and Axel's crumpled body on the floor. I can't tell where the blood is coming from, but it covers the whole of his face.

"What do you mean everything?" I ask, ignoring the shouts coming from the guys. I can see Axel's body still in a heap on the ground. The twist in my gut tells me I have to do something.

"The fortune. The town. Everything," he says with a smirk. "Sign it over to me so I have full control and then I will let you and the boys leave. If you don't, I'll make you watch as I kill them first."

He means it, I can tell with the set of his jaw – he wouldn't think twice at killing us. Knox and Frost scream at me, but I can't look at them, at the moment. My chin falls to my chest as I take slow deep breaths. Don't they realize they say they can't live in a world without me, but, similarly, I can't live in a world without them.

"I'll do it," I whisper. Defeat fills me but I have to. Nothing means more to me than they do.

"Bo, don't. He won't stick to his word," Frost pleads with me. I meet his gaze. The fight leaves him as he sees my resolve, and he knows there's no way he can talk me out of this.

"I have to. I can't save us any other way," I growl back, laugher fills the room. My head turns as my eyes narrow on the other people here. Titan's mother glares at me, her eyes filled with so much hatred – I don't break eye contact with her. If she hadn't popped out such a toxic bastard, then he may still be alive.

"You have until midnight to get everything sorted. If not, you know what we'll do," Adam says with a finality – like a door being slammed in my face. He clicks his fingers, and a figure comes out of the shadows. His face is stoic, but the size of him makes him not look real. He's like the size of the mountain from the TV show *Game of Thrones*. He strolls over, and I shuffle back a little - to put distance between us. He quirks a brow, and his eyes look over my guys. Groans fill the air, and I look to my right to see Axel stirring, when the chains drop off my wrists. My arms scream as I pull my hands forward and rub at the raw flesh on my arms. The pain makes me hiss as I see the rubbed flesh. My shoulders throb as I move them in small circles, trying to unlock the muscles there.

I pull myself up onto shaky legs, my knees feel like they're about to give way at any moment, but with sheer determination I manage to keep myself upright. I'm not falling in front of these fuckers. Adam walks over to me, my body tenses as his hand goes into the front of his suit jacket. He must see me tense because he smirks – he pulls his hand out and passes me my phone. My eyes narrow a touch as I take it, it's definitely my phone. The brute comes back, dropping some trainers on the floor. My eyes narrow as I realize it's a pair of mine from the cabin.

"Tick tock, Miss Walker," Adam growls, I stuff my feet in the trainers and tuck my arms under my armpits to keep my phone secure too. With one last look to the guys, chewing on my lower lip – I follow the brute. We've not even made it halfway across the warehouse when a door opens. My feet freeze in their spot as Kylo swaggers into the room with a shit-eating grin on his face.

"Leaving us so soon are we, Bo-Bo." His eyes look me over as I glare at the bastard. He examines the room a feral look taking over his face.

"Well, well look what we have here. The big bad Kenton Frost chained up like a little bitch," he sniggers, striding over to the guys. I turn my back on the brute keeping a close eye on him. "You're not so cocky now are you, brother?"

Frost's head lifts, his eyes taking in his twin. The hatred that shines on his face is obvious to everyone – it's easy to see how much he loathes him. Frost scoffs, turning away from him, a smirk tipping the edge of his lips. Axel and Knox both snigger too, keeping their eyes on each other.

"Don't turn away from me, you bastard," Kylo roars. The guys chuckle, and I can see Adam fighting back a smirk as he watches the younger one begin to vibrate with anger. I shoot forward, my feet eating up the ground just as he pulls back his fist. My body slams into him with enough force to knock him off his feet. I shove my forearm against his throat cutting off his airway with enough power to hold him in place.

"Touch my fucking men, while any of them are chained, you punk ass little bitch and I will rip your dick off and feed it to you," I snarl, the noise echoing in the empty space.

"This is why you will never beat him. If you have to go after your brother while he is chained, then you're as much of a dickhead as your father. And you know who holds the real power," the words snap with a finality, as I throw a punch into this jaw – just as I release my hold. Smirking as his ass drops to the floor on the other side of the column where his brother is sitting.

"If he touches any of them, Adam, the fucking deal is off." I turn my back on the little shit – I hear him growl at the disrespect. But I don't give a shit, I look to Adam and his demonic little wife, who looks like she wants to start shit. He stares back, but I don't break my eye contact – like fuck am I letting this shit slide.

"Deal," he grumbles, with a click of his finger another

brutish looking man strides into the room. Grabbing hold of an unconscious Kylo he drags his ass out of the room by the back of his t-shirt. With a curt nod, I follow the brute across the room to a door. I look over my shoulder – my eyes on my men. A grunt fills the air, I turn my attention back to the task at hand and follow like a good little girl. It doesn't take long until the brute points to another door, I stride down the corridor to what must be the exit. Throwing the door open, it bangs against the wall with force. The cold night air, slams into me. My breath clouding like a mist as a shiver washes over me, I scroll through the call list on my phone. Finding the one I want I hit the call button, and the line instantly starts ringing. As I shuffle from foot to foot, the cold settles into my body hardening it for what's about to come.

"Where are you?" I snap down the line, babbles filled with uncertainty are replied, making me snarl. "No! Stay where you are. I'm coming to you." I end the call abruptly. Opening the Uber app, I book a ride. I look over my shoulder and the piece-of-shit building as I wait for my ride. My chest tightens as I fight the urge to go back in there. I don't like the thought of them being in there on their own. If I go back, it's a sure way to kill us all, and we're not finished with our lives yet. These fuckers are about to see how far I'm willing to go to save the people I love.

CHAPTER TWENTY-THREE

Thank God the Uber app charges to your card or this would be a very awkward situation because, at the moment, I have zero money on me let alone any damn pockets. The look he gave me when he pulled up really got on my nerves, and throughout the drive over I knew he was fishing for information. He kept asking me if I ran away or if someone had hurt me. you would have thought the guy would've taken the hint after the fifth "mind your business" comment. But, no, Sir Lancelot here kept trying to be a knight in shining armor, asking me if I needed him to ring the police for me. I've been grinding my teeth for the last fifteen minutes, trying to distract myself because slamming my driver's head into his steering wheel wouldn't get me where I need to go in one piece.

The house comes into view, and I sigh with relief. The neighborhood is your typical suburban street with neat houses lining either side. All of them have some sort of SUV parked in the driveway. The car's brakes squeak as it rolls to a stop. I jump out before it comes to a full standstill. Throwing a grumbled thank you over my shoulder to the car, I march up the drive. Lifting my closed fist, I knock when I step up the single step to the front door. When it swings open, a pale-faced Mr. Geoffrey stares at me.

"Bo, what the fuck is going on?" he asks ushering me into the house – I'm surprised at the interior, and its all-open-plan living, the inside at war with the old-style look that's outside.

"Kylo has been working with Adam Black," I growl as a shudder passes over me, the cold well and truly settled into my bones now. I spot the decanter in the corner of a little nook, nestled on top of a small bookcase. I walk over grabbing a glass off the lower shelf. Mr. Geoffrey hasn't taken his eyes off of me since I came inside. Under his watchful gaze, I pour a full glass of the liquor, not bothering to smell it to find out what it is. The burn is instant as it burns a path down my throat, making me cough as it settles in my stomach, which rolls at the sensation from either a lack of food or water for the duration of time I was chained. Or maybe because there is still lingering alcohol and drugs in my system. Either way, I welcome the burn.

"What do you mean?" he asks, his eyes wide as he extends a hand for a glass of his own.

With a deep breath I give him the rundown on what's happened since the fire, watching as his face turns ashen the deeper I get into the story. He looked like he was going to be physically sick when I told him about me passing out with the drugs and was concerned that someone had done something to me. That thought had crossed my mind, but I don't think they did. The only one whom I think would have tried something like that is Kylo, but Frost turned up at the proper time to distract him or pull his attention away from me. Mr. Geoffrey hasn't said anything for ten minutes, his eyes meeting mine – then he diverts his gaze quicky.

"Mr. Geoffrey, I have to do something. They are going to kill them if I don't," I say with the unease growing again. He opens his mouth like a fish out of water, emotions flickering over his face like he's having some sort of internal war.

"There's so much going on that you don't know about, and I feel like I've deceived you by withholding the truth," he says with downcast expression. My eyes narrow on him as my unease turns into worry as I rack my brain.

"What the fuck are you on about?" I snap. "I need your fucking…." My words break off as a ping fills the room, along with my phone vibrating in my hand. Dread fills me as I see an unknown number on the screen, I press the message and an attachment comes up. But it's the words that have nausea swirling in my gut.

"Remember the clock is ticking, so we thought we would give you a little bit of motivation and a reminder not to try something stupid!" My whole hand trembles as my thumb hovers over the link, and with a deep breath I hit it. The video is dark at first, but then a scream splits the air. The video then pans out and all I can see at first is someone's shoes. The video lifts, my hands shake as I gasp – horror filling me as I realize it's Rafe on the screen, hanging from the rafters with chains around his wrists. His t-shirt is torn, and bruises and blood cover his face and body, his face is swollen in parts, but it doesn't matter I know it's him. Someone in a black ski mask swings a slugger again, and Rafe screams on impact, the sound making my knees buckle. Mr. Geoffrey yanks the phone out of my hand as I pant with tears rolling down my cheeks – they have him, we were hoping they didn't find him. But him not answering makes sense. How could he have when he was there?

"Fuck, Bo. I'm so sorry," Mr. Geoffrey blurts, as he rubs along his jaw with his knuckle "I told him it would go too far and that we should tell you what's been going on."

"What do you mean 'he'?" I demand as my anxiety spikes

and sweat begins to build on the back of my neck. He grimaces as my eyes track every slight little twitch his face makes – his chest rises and falls as he searches for somewhere to look other than at me.

"What. The. Fuck. Do. You. Mean. 'He'?" I growl, as I stalk forward. The fear on his face tells me that this shit is bad – his shoulders deflate as he takes a deep pained breath.

"I knew Frost was alive," he blurts, his tone having a slight tremble to it. My brows hit my hairline at the admission and then anger consumes me.

"You fucking knew?" I seethe, my whole body vibrates as the rage starts to swallow me whole. "You watched everything I went through, and you fucking knew?"

"He told me he would kill me if I told you. But he needed my help to keep you safe," he pleads, his voice shaking as he slumps onto a chair in the living room. "You know as well as I do, when he says something, he means it."

Hostility for the both of them fills me as I try to rein in my emotions. But what the actual fuck are both of them playing at? "I know what he's like, but what the actual fuck, Mr. Geoffrey? I trusted you," I spit.

"I know you did, and you don't realize how hard it was for me to keep this from you. But I had to as he was always breathing down my neck," he says with a soft tone. His face is pale, and the guilt is clear. My thumb and index finger press into my eyes as a headache starts to grow. I begin pacing, my breaths shallow as my mind runs rampant.

"Why would he want you to keep it from me?" I ask, my brows furrow as I pull my hair free from the hair tie – running my fingers through the length.

"He's been working in the background since he left," he admits with a harsh breath. "He wanted to make it up to you for all the pain he caused. Then, he got wind of someone making moves against you. So, Frost, being himself, he had to know your enemies to learn them."

"I can't deal with this now, I have to get everything sorted out. They're hurting Rafe, the guys are going through whatever the fuck is happening to them," I boom, my emotions spiraling.

"Do you really think they would hurt the others to get at you?" he asks with a look of horror. I lift my head, so our eyes meet. With a sharp nod he pales further – I never thought anyone could manage to pale as much as he has.

"After seeing the video, yeah. I think they would hurt the guys to, as they say, motivate me."

"Bo?" the words are soft, my focus zeros in on him chewing on his bottom lip as he rings his hands together. "I know there's a lot going on at the moment and this is the worst possible time, but you need to know."

My head swirls and my skin begins to itch as I watch him chew on his nails while he looks over me then averts his gaze. This only adds to my apprehension as I feel my veins chilling. After another beat of silence, "Spit it out, for fuck's sake."

"They found out the cause of the fire," he says, his lower lip trembles.

"Ok, that's a good thing," I reply with a pinched mouth and furrowed brows. Why is he so worried about telling me this.

"It was arson," he blurts, jumping to his feet as he starts pacing. He runs his hand over his head, as he looks to me, tears shining in his eyes.

"Ok. I thought as much but what the hell, Mr. Geoffrey?" I can't be dealing with half-truths or riddles. I chew on my lip as I fight back the growl that's building, I turn my back on him, grabbing my phone from the side.

"I found out the Blacks had something to do with it, but that's not what is killing me," he says, the sound is hollow. My teeth grind with enough force to have my jaw aching as I whirl around to face him.

"It was Ms. Jeanette."

My legs give way, I land with a thud. I feel a slight pain in my lower body but that's nothing compared to the pain of my heart shattering. A hiccup sob passes my lips. Tears fall from the edges of my eyes, as my mind conjures up the smell. My stomach rolls, the vision tormenting me, and pain rushes through every part of my body. It almost feels like the good that was left in my soul has been ripped out of me. My body trembles as the nausea builds. I close my hands into fists – pressing them into the floor on either side of me. Everything hits me like a tsunami, and I end up on my hands and knees. My fists pound into the tiles, and the wild feeling is feral as it continues to build within me. I see feet through my tear-filled eyes, but I'm only able to make out the shape as they stop in front of me. My fists spilt under the power of the blows, and I scream. Pouring everything into the sound - my anger, guilt, horror, and sickness. The sound filling the air is like the sound of a dying animal. They did this. They took away the one person who was keeping me rational. The one piece of my soul that made me want to be the person she always told me I could be. They took my men and me to gain something that never belonged to them.

"Bo?" A voice breaks through the wall of emotion, and my scream dies to nothing. I lift my head, my gaze meeting Mr. Geoffrey's. He takes a step back from me, his eyes wide as he holds his hands up in a frightened gesture. I grab my phone off the side, checking the time and I see its ten thirty. Which means I only have an hour and a half to get everything sorted.

"I need some clothes. Then, I need you to tell me everything Frost was working on," I command. His head bobs in a rapid nod as I make my way through the house to the spare room I know is on the bottom floor. I step through the door with the moonlight taunting me as it shines through the open curtains, bathing the room in its glow. I find the number I never thought I would be using and hit call. It only rings once.

"He's busy," a voice snaps on the other end of the line. I growl at the disrespect of this fuckwit.

"Get me fucking Reed. Now," I growl. The voice is silent for a second then a hurried apology is muttered.

"Reed," A gruff voice snaps, my teeth grind. At this rate I'm going to crack my teeth. "Who is this? I don't have time to play games."

"It's Bo," his gasp is harsh as the line goes silent for a minute. I pull the phone away from my ear making sure the call is still connected. "He needs you, and you owe me."

"When?" he asks a savage sound rumbling down the line.

"Now," I bark, the line goes quite again, but then orders are being barked out and I can hear the chaos from the other people as it turns into a frenzy.

"We'll be there in thirty minutes." I cut the call, just as Mr. Geoffrey knocks on the door. He comes in with a pile of clothes. I grab the black jeans, pushing my legs into them as he moves backwards.

"Reed and the boys will be here in thirty minutes," I growl, his feet stop moving as his brows hit his hairline. "Now tell me how far Frost got with his plan."

It didn't take long for Mr. Geoffrey to fill me in on the plan that Frost was coming up with but didn't have enough information to be able to finish it off. While I was getting ready, much to his horror, we found out everything and put a plan into place. Now we're at the island waiting, and the bell rings as I start to lose my patience.

"Took you long enough," I snarl, as footsteps fill the air and I see the huge, tattooed guy stroll into the house with no fucks given. "Make no mistake, Reed. If you fuck this shit up, I will fuck your life up."

"Damn, he wasn't joking when he said you could be savage," he jests with a chuckle. I look the goon up and down, the arrogance that oozes off him explains a lot. I chuckle. Then, a smirk tips the edge of my lips.

"Now I know where he gets his dickish attitude from," I throw back and he laughs a deep belly laugh as he nods.

"Watch your fucking mouth, bitch," one of the other guys further behind snaps, his eyes raking over me with disgust. A few others laugh too.

"Yo, Reed, what the fuck are we doing here with the pampered princess?" another shouts his annoyance as the others nod their heads in agreement.

"Watch your mouth. This is Axel's girl," Reed snarls back trying to bring his men back in line, I slide off the stool – Mr. Geoffrey's head whips side-to-side as he watches the back-and-forth like a tennis match.

"So fucking what? Boss isn't around anymore because he jumped ship for some rich bitch gash," the first guy shouts back. Reed snarls turning on his man. I place my hand on his arm. His head drops to the contact, his brow furrowing. I smirk at him, and he chuckles as he steps back.

"Rich bitch?" I chuckle as I look over the group of guys that are filling Mr. Geoffrey's house, at the moment. I look over to the one who protests the most, my eyes taking in every scrawny little detail of him. He's skinnier than most of them, and the way he holds himself tells me he's a little boy playing "hard man" with the others. I lash out, my fist connecting with his nose as a satisfying crunch fills the air. I smile manically as blood pours from his nose. I throw another punch hitting him square in the jaw and he crumbles onto his knees in front of me.

"I am not a rich bitch," I snap, gripping hold of the back of his head and tilting his head back so he's forced to look up at me. "I came from nothing. I grew up with a normal life, and I never wanted any of this, but unfortunately, the name I hold brought this shit onto my shoulders. So, make a shitty judgement once more, and I'll make sure you're eating food through a tube for the rest of your life." A round of "oh fucks" fill the air as the others take a small step back. I hear Reed chuckle darkly behind me, and poor Mr. Geoffrey is shaking at the other side of the room.

"Do I make myself clear?" I demand, yanking him back further until he winces with the pain that I know is radiating up his neck.

"Crystal," he hisses through clenched teeth, I let go and he falls onto his arse. His eyes darken as the others start laughing, and I lift a brow. Folding my arms across my chest, my leather jacket makes the horrid noise it does when the material rubs together. I wait to see if this idiot is going to run his mouth again, but I've got a lot of pent-up shit I need to expel. He pulls to his feet, his eyes running over me. Then, his eyes connect with mine and a wide smile spreads across his face.

"Now that's sorted, this is what I need you to do."

CHAPTER TWENTY-FOUR

"Stop fidgeting, Mr. Geoffrey," I bark, as he shuffles from foot-to-foot beside me. I can feel the anxiety rolling off him in waves and it's really starting to piss me off. The ticking clock is loud in the office, which pushes my unease through the roof. My fingers drum on the desk as I keep checking my phone waiting for a response, but nothing has come through. The lift dings with the doors opening in a flourish.

"Glad to see you're doing the right thing, Bo," Adam purrs as he strolls in closely followed by his wife and Novack. "Forgive my eagerness but this is a long time coming and we're in a hurry to get it over with."

"I want to confirm my guys are ok before I do anything?" I demand from my seat behind the desk, and I smirk as his eyes narrow at the disrespect I'm showing. I don't break eye contact, waiting for him to do as I've asked. I see his jaw tick, as he clicks his fingers. Novack, the little pansy, searches his suit jacket for a few seconds, then he pulls out a phone. Passing it to Adam whose fingers fly across the screen, the phone going to his ear, he commands whoever is on the line to do a video call to show me the guys. He ends the call, and it rings again.

He answers the phone, and striding over to the desk, he slides the phone across the top. My heart skips a beat as I see all four of them together. The only ones with any damage are Axel and Rafe who thankfully have been chained together. Axel tries to soothe Rafe. Seeing the pain he's in is like a knife straight to my heart. Axel doesn't look any better with all the swelling on his face. My teeth grind as I see Frost, Knox and Deacon – sitting there with angry looks on their faces. I can see the shivers wash over them with the cold.

"Let's get this shit over with," I demand, pushing to my feet. I look to Mr. Geoffrey, and he tugs at the edge of his collar. The feel in the room has all of us on edge. He scuttles to the other side of the room, grabbing the file for me. He brings it over, his gaze on me. His face is wild with emotion. I smile softly to reassure him, and he blows out a breath.

"Why are you so nervous, Mr. Geoffrey?" Novack demands, his eyes flicking from me to him.

"He doesn't agree with what I'm doing. Isn't that right, Mr. Geoffrey?" I say. He nods his head in acknowledgement. Adam's eyes narrow. "Oh, cut the shit, Adam, what did you think would happen? I'm doing as you've asked. So, let's keep the hostility to a minimum, shall we?"

I open the folder, my pen scratching against it as I scribble my signature on all the pages with the tabs. The last signature done, I lift my head, and extend the pen to Adam whose smile is vicious. He looks at the pen in disgust, pushing his hand into the front of his jacket, he pulls out one of his own. I chuckle at the ego on him, as I notice the gold pen with an engraving on the top of it. He's as flamboyant as a peacock fluffing its feathers so I shouldn't be shocked to see this asshole has a solid gold pen. It's just another way for him to rub the peasants' noses in it.

"It's real, you know," he muses as he finishes up signing his name where he needs to. I lift a brow. "The pen. I just think it adds to the look I want to give off."

"It looks a little gaudy for my liking, but to each his own and all that," I retort with a chuckle. I pick up the file and pull out both lots of paper. He watches me intently as I put them into separate piles. I hand him his copies and pass off my own to Mr. Geoffrey who scampers away to the filing cabinet.

"Well, pleasure doing business with you, Bo," he beams, offering his hand for me to shake. I look at it like it's a sleeping lion waiting to chew my hand off. I force a smile taking his offered hand. He frowns at this but pulls it back with a chuckle. Novack stands at the back with a triumphant grin on his face, and Adam's wife looks like she's sucking on a lemon with her pinched features. They all turn on their heels, striding towards the lift with long confident strides – I stalk them two steps behind. Mr. Geoffrey is behind me a step as I look over my shoulder. His eyes are dancing with excitement as I smirk. The door dings and I rush forward holding the door to keep them from closing.

"What're you doing?" Adam booms from inside the metal box. I grin savagely as I look over the occupants.

"I have a question for you and Novack," I muse, my eyes bouncing between them. "Which one of you decided to kill my grandparents and parents?" I enquire with a cocked head, taking every slight twitch into account.

"I have no idea what you're talking about," he snaps, his cheeks tinging pink - he pulls at the tie that's around the collar. My smile widens as I see Novack shuffling in the background.

"Ah, you see that's where I know that is bullshit," I growl, my hand trembling on the lift door. "You see some amazing information just so happened to pop up in a file I found and well there's a special place in hell for people like you." I lunge forward ripping the paperwork out of his hand. A malicious smile spreads as his eyes widen as I shred it to pieces just as the doors close. Yells echo from within, I turn to face Mr. Geoffrey – his expression matches mine as I hear a grinding, then a crunch and screams.

"I think it's best we take the stairwell."

CHAPTER TWENTY-FIVE

FROST

"How's he doing, Axel?" I ask with a hushed tone. We've been talking as quietly as we can since they dragged an unconscious Rafe into the room with us. The devastation that hit us when we realized they managed to get their hands on him was gut-wrenching.

"I'm not a doctor," he snaps, his face lined with concern. Rafe is slumped against the column – his bindings are in front of him with a length of chain going through the one that's wrapped around the stone, keeping Axel in his place.

"Do you think Bo's ok?" Deacon's voice echoes, and all of our heads whip around to see him. *Shit.* I forgot he was here with us, he was so quiet. "She will be, won't she?"

"She's tougher than anyone gives her credit for," Knox breathes with a smile on his face, and I chuckle at the wistful look. I still remember the state of him after she beat his ass that day in the gym – I don't know who was more shocked; us or him.

"She's up to something," Axel whispers, trying to keep his voice low so he doesn't catch the guards' attention. "Think about it, when has she ever given up that easily?"

His words sink in as my eyes widen. He's right. She would never bow like that to anyone, and she did. I'm pretty sure Knox's face matches mine as we stare at each other. "You think the guards are still listening?"

"No, brother. They aren't," the slimy voice of Kylo echoes through the air. I hear Axel growl, and Knox sits up straighter as Deacon moves himself further round so we are all facing each other.

"Your little girlfriend isn't here to save your ass this time, is she?" He chuckles, stepping out of the shadows with an evil glint in his eyes.

"Well, you haven't done your research that well, then, brother because she is my wife," I boom, my anger taking over. It's meaningless because I'm tied up – but it does make me feel a little better. He bursts out laughing, deep booming belly laughs, as he doubles over.

"Dude?" Knox says, his eyes trained on me. I try to read the expression on his face, but I can't. "The wedding wasn't real."

"The fuck you talking about?" My voice squeakier than I would have liked. *What the fuck*?

"Daddy well fucked you over big brother," Kylo laughs again. My brows furrow in confusion as I look between my friends.

"I don't like the fucker, bro, but he's right. Bo didn't go into too much detail, but she found out that the wedding was faked. It never truly happened," Knox's face drops as my mind races to try figure out what the fuck his endgame was.

"What the fuck do you mean it wasn't real!" My voice booms, echoing off the walls, the guys wince as I feel my world teetering on the edge.

"You're full of shit," I round on my so-called brother, who's grinning at me like this is the best shit he's seen. "Take off my restraints and say it to my face you fucker."

His eyes widen a little, but I feel the beast within rushing to the surface. If that bastard wasn't dead already, I would kill him. *She is mine*!

"She's still ours, regardless," Deacon says, his face imploring me to stay calm at the new piece of information. My mind races as my skin becomes taut. I tug on my bindings trying, with all the strength I have, to break me out. After five minutes of grunting the only thing I've managed is to rub my wrists raw.

Take deep breaths, don't let him see that this is bothering you. I should have known he would find a way to fuck me over. *Hang on*! This makes sense now, if we were never married, he didn't have anything standing in his way and that's why he took her.

"Kylo, fucking help us!" A voice bellows from somewhere further down. His head whips around as screams and yells fill the air.

"Kylo, don't be a little bitch," the guy who led Bo out of here earlier bellows as he falls through the door with a someone I've never seen. Kylo takes off in the opposite direction as me and the guys shuffle in our spots as chaos echoes all around us.

"Argh," Kylo's body slides across the floor, stopping in front of me – his head rolling to the side. "Now, fuckface, where do you think you're going?" A blonde-haired guy says with a savage smile on his face.

"Ace?" Axel breathes with a laugh. "What the fuck are you doing here?" My head tilts to the side, as my lips purse – studying the newcomer with a keen sort of interest.

"We've had orders to rescue your asses," he says with a dark chuckle, he yanks a limp Kylo off the floor – without any care at all. Seeing him being handled like that brings a demonic smile to my face. *But oh, how I wish it was me doing it to the little fucker*.

"Orders of who?" Axel demands, his brows pinched together as he looks deeper into the warehouse.

"Boss lady," he grumbles rubbing under his eye that is bruised, wincing as he presses a little too hard on the wound. "You could have warned us she's a psycho," he growls, slamming the body down into a chair and tying him to it.

"She do that?" Axel asks with a chuckle as he nods to the bruise lining the length of his jaw. The guy named Ace grunts, and the noise has Axel bursting out laughing, his shoulders bouncing as the laughter gets louder. "I always told you that your mouth would get you into trouble."

"Ha. Ha," He rolls his eyes, finishing his task without another word to any of us.

"Any chance you're planning on unchaining us anytime soon, asshat?" Knox growls, he switches his position again the best he can but with the size of him, he's finding it hard to get into a position he's comfortable in.

"Patience isn't your strong suit is it, brawler?" and Knox growls as Ace grins at him like the milky bar kid, shooting gun fingers into the air. Axel laughs, and Deacon and I snigger as we watch Knox turn bright red with rage.

"What's the plan with him?" I ask, Ace shrugs looking between me and the one I share a face with. "Ok, I guess it's time my brother and I have a little chat."

The cocky little fuck scoffs then, and I roll my eyes. Jesus, I never realized how arrogant we were. *I wonder if we're wired wrong because of the dickhead*? A throat clearing has me looking over my shoulder, and I see the guys all look at me with confused expressions. My eyes land on Rafe widening as I see he's slumped against Axel. He holds his ribs with his free arm, and his eyes are so swollen they are mere slits. His eyes are on Kylo, and rage is clear even with the state he's in. I give a curt nod and they head off deeper into the space, giving us a chance to talk on our own.

"How did you find out about me?" I ask, the question has been at the front of my mind since I found out who he was.

"Jamieson told me when I was ten," he barks, his teeth gnashing together like an animal.

"Why the fuck were you with Jamieson? I heard the security mention him growing up. He was dad's most trusted man."

"Why don't you ask daddy dearest?" he barks. "Oh, wait you can't because your toxic bit of pussy killed him." I lunge, gripping him by the throat, squeezing until it looks like his eyes are going to pop out of his head, and fear flashes across his face.

"Let's get one thing fucking straight," I growl in his face. "Bo didn't kill dad. I did." His head draws back, his eyes wide. I smirk at the fear that spreads across his face once more. "I did warn you in the courtyard that you made a mistake in going after her," I say with a smirk. "He learnt that lesson the hard way."

"You killed your own blood for her?" he asks his eyes wide, his tone trembling slightly. He coughs to clear his throat, and I chuckle darkly.

"I'd kill you for her if I had to," I say with a shrug, and he reels back. The chair tips backwards, and I put my foot on the plastic, forcing it back onto four legs. "But I know how toxic this environment is, and I don't really want to put mother through another loss."

"Mom's dead," he roars, lunging forward. "You're a sick fucker for lying about something like that."

"Who told you she was dead?" I watch the confusion spread across his face as he glares at me, "Look you have no reason to trust me, but I don't want to have to do something drastic if I don't have to." He studies me as I do the same thing, both of us trying to get a read on each other.

"Jamieson did," he says with a whisper. "He told me she died giving birth to us." He blows out a harsh breath, his face is pale as he stares at me with wide eyes.

"How did you get involved with Adam Black?" I growl, pushing away from him as I rub my chin deep in thought. His reactions don't make sense, and why the fuck would my dad allow his man to tell his son his that mother was dead?

"Jamieson was a Black." My heart skips a beat, as my veins buzz. I turn in a slow circle, and Bo strides through the room, with Mr. Geoffrey and a huge, tattooed guy a step behind. Her face is stoic and body tense as her gaze is pinned on him.

"Bo-Bo?" She looks like my girl, but the cold look on her face isn't the girl I love. This girl is completely devoid of emotion. Deacon and Knox step towards her, but Mr. Geoffrey halts them with a shake of his head.

"They used him as a puppet feeding him false lies. Training him to do what nobody else could do," she says with a harsh crack, and I wince at the sound. She stops beside me, but her eyes never meet mine.

She steps forward, Kylo's eyes widen as he tries to shuffle his chair back. The hostility rolling of her is infectious as the movement in the area stops. All the members of the Knights stop. I look over my shoulder to Axel, who's in a staring contest with the tattooed guy. He shakes his head, and Axel's chin drops to his chest. A thud echoes around the room, and my head whips around. I step forward on instinct as Bo places her foot on Kylo's throat.

"You made a serious fuck up, coming after me arsehole," she rumbles, crouching down so her weight presses harder onto him with her full weight. "I should end your fucking life now for what you took away from me. You took the only thing I had close to family."

"Ms. Jeanette," I gasp as realization dawns on me. My gaze connects with Mr. Geoffrey, and he nods. My chest clenches as I look back to her, I can see her hands trembling as she tries to keep everything together. That's the thing about her, she wouldn't allow anyone to see her break, she would see it as showing weakness.

"Did you know the plan was to set my house on fire?" she demands. Kylo gasps as he opens his mouth to speak. Bo stands up, removing her foot, and he starts coughing, but that doesn't make a difference because she grabs the front of his top pulling him up to sitting with more power than I knew she had. "Answer me!"

"No," he croaks between coughs. "I was told we had a job and to follow a couple of the guys and help out if needed. So, I went along not questioning the order."

"Then, what?" she demands, her arms folded across her chest, and there's a savage beauty to her right now.

"I realized where we were once we were in the garden. I didn't know what they were doing, but one of the guys ran off and then the next thing I know flames were devouring one side of the house," he answers with a defeated tone. "I had no idea the plan was to burn it down. I ran then, and when I got out onto the street, I pulled my hood up and waited. Then, I saw them pull out a body." She growls a feral sound then, both Mr. Geoffrey and the other guy step back. "I didn't mean for anyone to die. I'm so sorry."

An ear-splitting scream fills the air, and I duck as the sound reverberates of the stone walls. She lashes out with a fist, hitting him in the jaw. The sound intensifies, she punches him again. The sound is demonic as it builds in volume. Anguish and pain fill the noise as she lands blow after blow. He doesn't make a sound as he takes everything she has to give until her blows slow and she pulls back panting.

"I want to know everything," she growls, her whole body shaking with all the emotions she's feeling. "I won't kill you because I know that's what she would tell me to do. She always saw the things we couldn't see, and you've been used in a sick and twisted game. I won't destroy her memory like that."

He nods, blood trickling down his face from the various wounds her blows have just made. He takes a deep breath and starts talking. We all listen intently as the story deepens, and the guys move closer to listen, too.

I have no words for the story I've just heard. They've lied to him all his life about almost everything. The only thing that doesn't surprise me, if it's true, is my father saying to Jamieson that he didn't have need for the son who killed his wife. He was a vile man and the fact he could make a bullshit story up like that, well, the man was truly evil, and the world is a little better without him in it. Bo reacted badly to some of the stuff that was said about the plans they were making, so they could take over. She had to walk off, but it wasn't long before she came back with her emotions under control. They told him that her family were to blame for everything and that's why they made the deaths look like accidents.

"Bo?" I say, the question has been burning the back of my throat for some time now. "What happened to Adam and the others?"

She barks out a laugh, the sound is harsh as she grins manically. "They went splat," she says with a chuckle. "You can never fully trust things and unfortunately for them the lift had an accidental impact in the foyer."

The tattooed guy I now know is called Reed looks to her with wide eyes. He chuckles then shakes his head, like he can't believe the way she's just described the incident.

"So, what happens now?" Kylo asks with unease, his eyes bouncing between us all.

"I don't want you anywhere in my town," she replies, turning to me. "You got any ideas?"

"I think he should go to mom," I say. I see his head shoot up as he stares at me. "I think it would do him some good to get to know her, and with some luck he might be able to bring her back."

"Looks like you're going to Broad Creek. I'll be honest," she says her eyes on my brother. Some of the tension has left her since he started talking. "I still want to see you pay, but you were led astray by others who wanted to use you for their own gain," she takes a deep breath. "Use this opportunity to change and become better than the blood that runs in your veins."

"I promise. I can't tell you how sorry I am for everything. I know it will never be enough. But I will do this," he says as he meets my gaze. I can see the truth of the words shining in his eyes. I just hope he sticks to it.

CHAPTER TWENTY-SIX

M y arse is numb from the drive over to Broad Creek. It's another rich person's town just two hours away. The emotional rollercoaster it's been has only added to the swell of emotions I'm still reeling from. Danica was so overcome with emotion when she saw Kylo that I couldn't help but smile at her reaction. She and the boys talked for ages, and Kylo has agreed he wants to stay with her to get to know her and have a fresh start. There's still no word from Axel on how Rafe is doing, and we're all eager to get back and find out what's happening. I really need to catch up with Mr. Geoffrey, too, and see if I can sort us out another house as soon as possible.

"I've got us covered on that one Bo-Bo," Frost grins from the driver's seat. I look behind me to Knox and Deacon – both of them shrug in response to my silent question.

"Did you learn to read minds while you were playing dead?" I ask bewildered. He barks out a laugh, palm slapping against the wheel as we continue on our way back.

"You spoke out loud, again," he replies, chuckling. My brows lift as I look back to the other two – who are smirking in the back seat. My cheeks heat as embarrassment roars to life. *Fuck my life – why do I always say the stuff out loud*? "There's no need to be embarrassed," he chuckles. "We find it adorable." All three of them burst out laughing as my cheeks flame brighter, and I smack him in the back of the head. He shouts "ow," dramatically, as he narrows his eyes on me.

"Fucking adorable," I growl folding my arms. "I brought you fuckers to your knees, didn't I?" I smirk, as all of them fake gasp with their eyes wide as I look between them all.

"But you're so cute," Knox chuckles from behind me, patting me on the head. I smirk, leaning forward to get out of reach from his hand, I pull the adjuster and the seat slides back – he yelps as I pin his legs. The other two burst out laughing as he squeals like a pig because he can't move.

"That's what you get for being a condescending fuck," I chuckle as he pushes on the back rest.

"Bo, c'mon! This fucking hurts, gorgeous" he pleads with me. I cackle louder – stretching out my legs with a sigh. He growls, the sound only adding to my amusement.

"So, you think he's going to change now that he's with your mom?" Deacon asks.

"I hope so. She was so happy to see him. I've never seen so much emotion from her," Frost replies, his tone low. I think he's a little pissed that she had a reaction like she did to seeing Kylo. Don't get me wrong, she was ecstatic to see that Frost was alive, but angry that he didn't tell her the plan. She understood after some explaining, but when she saw Kylo she lost it. I managed to explain to Frost that it wasn't because she loved Kylo more, but because she had eighteen years thinking he died at birth. We told Kylo we would check in often, and if he needed anything all he had to do was reach out to his brother.

I really want to be supportive but it will take time after

everything has happened. However, I know this is what Ms. Jeanette would have wanted. Mr. Geoffrey sent me a text saying he managed to get in touch with her family and they asked if they could have her ashes, but they did agree to allowing me to have some. He also passed on my message to them to not worry about money issues as I will be taking over what she was sending them each month. She thought I didn't know, but I did. I saw the transaction one day by accident. She was sending three quarters of the money I was paying her to them. This is the least I can do for much she became a part of my family. I want to make sure her memory lives on and her family is taken care of.

"Hey, Axel, how's he doing?" Frost's voice pulls me out of my inner thoughts. I see Axel's name on the screen, and my anxiety spikes as the other end of the line is quiet.

"He's ok. He's got two broken ribs and cuts and bruising. Doc said he's lucky he doesn't have a concussion. So, all-in-all, he's ok," relief washes over me, and my body sags into the seat as I share a look with Frost. I hear both guys exhale from the back. Anxiety has been riding us all hard as we waited for news.

"How did it go with your mom? How's Majesty doing?" the rumble of his voice soothes me. After seeing Adam beating him and with what they did to Rafe their deaths were too quick for my liking.

"She's happier now that she knows you're both ok," Frost answers. Axel chuckles - the sound is refreshing after the chaos. "Kylo should be ok."

"Hey, Axel," I blurt cutting Frost's words off. Everyone laughs as I glare at the dick beside me and he just smirks. "Did Mr. Geoffrey manage to get everything sorted with the police?"

"Yeah, it's all good, Majesty, you don't need to worry," he says with another chuckle. "Ok, asshole, I'll ask her," he growls at someone. "Reed wants to know if you'd be up for keeping the Knights in line when they piss him off?"

I laugh, a deep sound that comes straight from my stomach. It doesn't help when I hear loads of bickering coming from his end of the line. "Tell Reed that's not a problem, but then he needs to remember he owes me."

"Thanks, savage," Reed's voice booms through the speakers. "Oh, and remember if you want any more ink you need to come and see me."

"Not a fucking chance are you tattooing her!" Four voices roar. Reed chuckles darkly and I join in. *Haven't they realized yet, I do what I want when I want?*

"How long do you think he'll be in for?" Frost asks Axel as I'm still giggling at their outburst.

"We're waiting for the papers so he can sign himself out," Axel replies.

"Good, I'll text you an address. Meet us there," Frost commands.

"Got it." The line goes dead, and I look over to Frost whose concentration is steadfast on the road. I try to read him but he's as closed off as he normally is.

"You can study me all you want B0-Bo, but you're getting nothing out of me. It's a surprise," I groan. I fucking hate surprises – they all know that. He laughs like the dick he is, the sound being echoed by two more.

I yawn as I see it's four in the morning, and tiredness washes over me – I pull my seat forward. Knox blows out a sigh of relief, and I get myself comfortable with my arm under my head on the door. I feel my eyes start to close, the void pulling me into the belly of it.

I wake, unwillingly from the deep sleep I was in, with a jolt to the sound of doors slamming. "Where're we?" I croak, my throat as dry as the desert.

"Sorry Bo-Bo, but it's time for your surprise," Frost says, his breath brushing against my ear. I turn my head, his lips connect with mine. He growls deeply, and the sound is like a balm to my soul. I break the contact and push myself up from the door, I see trees surrounding us. I look behind me and it's the same out of the back window too.

"Where are we?" I ask, my brain still fuzzy.

"Come see," he says with a happy tone. I narrow my eyes on him, and the smile that spreads across his face is gorgeous. I rack my brain to remember if I've ever seen him smile like that, but I come up empty. I fumble with my seatbelt - my fingers not working right the first two tries. The click fills the car on my third attempt, and I climb out of the car. My mouth drops open as the lake stretches to my left. The sun is breaking over the mountains, and the birds are singing as the first signs of sunrise happen.

I turn in a circle taking everything in, and see that there's a road weaving a path through the trees that we must have just driven down. The lake and the mountains surrounding this place are my idea of heaven – my eyes land on the guys all staring at me with huge smiles on their faces. It's what's behind them that captures all of my attention, though, and my mouth drops open.

The cabin is a two-story black building with glass windows at every possible point. A huge balcony spreads around one side with double doors that must lead to a bedroom. A deck, fully illuminated by some lights, sits off to the right side, with a hot tub on it. On the left is a path that leads down to the lake. The path is surrounded by a huge set of rose bushes – one bright crimson red and the other yellow. A tear leaks from the corner of my eye as emotions crash into me. I open my mouth to speak but nothing comes out.

"Do you like it?" Frost asks nervously. My eyes connect with his and I can see the worry. I rush forward, diving into his arms, as the tears roll down my cheeks.

"How did you do this?" I ask between sobs, everything just feels too much, at the moment.

"I started building it for myself," he says with a soft tone. "I got the idea from Ms. Jeanette when she was telling me about her perfect home one day. But I added my own tweaks to it."

"I love it," I croak as I slide down his front. The others are looking at me with huge smiles on their faces. "She would've loved to see this," I say as another sob escapes.

"That's why I had my men add the roses. I know she loved coming to the lake when she had a chance." My brows hit my hairline as I realize how much thought he put into this. "Mr. Geoffrey added her ashes so she is where she loved to be, but also so she's a part of our lives, too."

Tears stream down my face as I pull away, taking slow steps towards the yellow roses – I know were her favorite. I see a plaque sticking out of the ground just under the flowers. Her name is etched in gold, and I smile as a gust of wind brushes over me. The feeling warms me a little, and it's like she's telling me everything is ok.

"What does this place feel like to you?" Axel asks me. I look over my shoulder with tear-stained cheeks. A wide smile stretches across my face as I look at all my men here.

"Home."

EPILOGUE

"**O**h fuck," I chant as the feeling of being so full has my head spinning. Frost pounds into my core while Deacon fucks my arse, and they both thrust into me with a brutality that has had me screaming with release more than once already. Deacon chuckles, as the grunts and moans get louder, and Knox grips my head turning it to a painful angle as his thrusts shallow in my mouth. My eyes land on Rafe and Axel fucking like their life depends on it, with both their eyes on me as I'm being railed by the others. Seeing them like this and having the others here has another rush of liquid coming.

"Fuck my life. She's so wet," Frost growls. As his thrusts pick up in pace, his brows crease in concentration.

"That's because she loves watching them," Deacon rumbles from below me. I clamp down on the both of them, pulling a guttural moan from them. Knox chuckles as I nod the best I can around his length, and he takes the opportunity to push further into my mouth. Both Rafe and Axel cum with a roar, and the sound has me clenching again.

"Oh fuck! You're soooo tight," Frost moans as he tries to thrust even harder. Deacon moans below me. His movements aren't as harsh as Frost's but the difference is sending my body into overdrive. I see Axel climb off the bed and disappear out of view. I cough as Knox impales me on his shaft - his pubic hairs tickling my nose. He holds me there until tears leak from the corners of my eyes.

Rafe comes into view with a smirk tipping the edge of his lips. The bruising is vicious today, but he said he wasn't missing out on this. He grabs my hand guiding it to his shaft, and bending my fingers around it in a firm grip as he starts to thrust his hips. His head rolls back with a moan. Fresh air invades my nose, and I suck down as much as I can as the tingles roar through my body. The bed dips and Axel kneels on my other side, and he does the same as Rafe. Frost's and Deacon's moans are growing more erratic along with my own - sweat coats me as the building orgasm has my limbs trembling. White dots speckle in front of my eyes as the chorus of moans lets me know we're all close. As Frost pounds into my core and Deacon fucks my arse, I jerk off both Rafe and Axel, while Knox skull fucks me. I've never felt so complete as I do right now. My orgasm explodes - my vision blacking out for a second as my body violent trembles. I scream around Knox's length, and the vibration sends him over the edge as his hot cum shoots down my throat. I swallow it down eagerly, swirling my tongue around the head as he extracts himself. Frost and Deacon roar as they are overcome by their release, and Rafe and Axel moan as thick white jets land on my stomach. Frost pulls out first, pulling me into a sitting position which has grunts coming from both Deacon and me. He continues to lift me up gently causing Deacon to slide out of my arse. I'm a trembling, panting mess as he lifts me off the bed and onto the floor, keeping a firm hold of me as he drops a kiss onto my forehead.

"You ready for today?" he asks, his eyes searching mine. I

hear the guys moving around behind me. All of them protested at the plan I have for today, but this is the best thing to do – it needs to be done.

"Yeah, I am. We best get ready," I say, pulling away. My legs are trembling a little, but I manage to keep myself upright. Frost and Axel smirk at this as I make my way to the bathroom.

"Quick question," Frost says as I make it to the door, and I turn slightly to see him. "How did you know about Rafe and Axel?" Both guys' cheeks tinge red. We weren't sure what was going to happen when he found out but he didn't react like we thought he might.

"I see more than I let on, Frost. All I want is for us all to be happy," I say, my eyes raking down length of his body. "Plus, it's hot as fuck watching them or when it's the three of us," I say with a wide smile. He barks out a laugh, shaking his head, as I see the tension leave the guys. "We need to hurry I want this shit ended today."

They nod their heads in unison, taking off in different directions as I make my way into the bathroom. I turn on the shower, then pull out my towels from the rack. My uniform is already on the chair waiting for me.

We all got ready in record time as I had the quickest shower known to man – I didn't bother with the usual routine I've had since coming here. My hair is towel dried and twisted into a messy bun on top of my head, my face is free from makeup, and I have my trusty combat boots on my feet. The guys wolf-whistled and cat-called as I came down the stairs, making me blush - much to their amusement. With a look to the guys, they

217

all smile at me as they climb into Knox's jeep, and I climb into the passenger seat of Frost's car.

He's already behind the wheel, and as his eyes meet mine, I nod, and the engine rumbles to life. I have just secured my belt when he peels out onto the road with the jeep following closely behind us, and we pull out onto the main road. Frost takes the corners too fast for my liking, and he just laughs every time I glare at him. The drive only takes us thirty minutes before the bustle of the town engulfs us. Drivers honk at cars that haven't taken off fast enough for them, and the streets are alive with people going about their lives. We pull into the academy lot, and the campus is alive with the student body – Frost sent a mass message out last night before we passed out telling them to be here before the teachers arrived.

That's why we're here at the ass crack of the day - to end this shit once and for all, and make sure the students know exactly what happens when you go against one of us. The guys climb out of the Jeep first, and whispers start as they move as one in front of the car. Frost climbs out next, and the student body go nuts seeing him here. With a deep breath I climb out, and the whispers get louder. With a look to the guys, I take off – my strides long as I head to the football field at the back of the academy. The chatter follows as I look over my shoulder to my men a step behind, and the rest of the school following behind, hot on their heels. I turn back, my pace picking up as I walk into the centre of the field. Gasps fill the air as they notice the unknowns sitting in the bleachers. Most of the guys stop behind me with Frost stopping at my side – his hand a comfort on my lower back as the students gather in front of us.

"You all know the shit that's happened since I came to this school," my voice booming. The noise settles down and all eyes turn to me. I smirk as I see Wankstein front and centre. She nods and I return the gesture. I hear a whispered "what the fuck" from Frost, and I have to hold back the smirk that is tipping my lips.

"The way some of you turned is shocking because loyalty is an important trait, not just in this school but also in the town," I say, and over half of the students nod their heads in agreement while others pale. "Now," the command booms.

Gasps fill the air as the crowd turns wild, some whooping as others look horrified. The crowd parts and Reed and Ace lead a man and woman out from the back of the crowd until they're facing me. The man's chin is on his chest while the woman stands with her head tipped up looking down the length of her nose at me, even though tears carve a path down her cheeks.

"What the fuck are you doing!" A high-pitched screech echoes, and my lips lift with a demonic smile. "Why have you brought them here," Jade screams, rushing to her father's side. Reed kicks the man in the back of the legs, forcing him onto his knees. The woman sobs as her husband doesn't make a sound.

"I defended you and brought a shitstorm down on myself," I say with a snap as I walk towards her. She stands to her full height, rushing forward to meet me head on. Her chest rising and falling rapidly. "This would have gone a different way, but I know this way will hit you harder than the other thing I had planned."

"What the fuck are you going to do?" she spits the words like a poison dart. "You're a nobody! A fucking waste of space." I chuckle at her outburst as growls fill the air, and the other students take a step back from my guys.

"I protected you like family," I growl forcing her back with a step. "I thought you were a friend. But that wasn't the case was it, Jade?" She breaks eye contact with a shudder visible to everyone. "You've been feeding the Blacks information since day one, hoping that Titan would have you as his Queen when he eventually took over the town."

Chaos erupts as the student body lose their shit over this. I raise my hand and the noise dies down again. I put my hand into my blazer pocket, and with precision, I pull out my knife. Her eyes widen. The blade pierces her skin before she even has chance to move. I grip the back of her neck holding her in place as Frost pins her hands down. The blade cuts like butter as a I carve a huge 'X' into her cheek, and blood flows from the wound like little rivers of crimson. I push her back with enough force to make her land on her arse next to her dad. Her mother screams as her father mutters "I'm sorry," and she whimpers – holding her face.

"You and your family are exiled from the town. Your businesses have been liquidated along with everything else," the students stare wide eyed as I pass out her judgment. "You are marked, which will tell anyone of importance that you are a traitor and can't be trusted."

"You can't do this to us!" She screams as two of the other Knights drop rucksacks in front of them. "We're an original family to this town."

"I am the original family name. Your family, along with others, got your leg up here because of my family. So I have every right to do with you as I please. Trust me when I say this is the lesser of two evils," I smile wildly as her eyes widen. "Now get the fuck out of my town."

Reed and Ace let go of her parents, and they scramble to pick up the rucksacks. Their eyes meeting mine, I feel the guys press in closer to be like a protective wall at my back. Jade's dad grabs hold of her arm, dragging her through the crowd as her mother follows closely behind. We don't take our eyes of off them until they are at the far side of the field.

"Reed, make sure they leave the town limits will you please," I ask the guy who has become a friend to the rest of us.

"You got it, Bo," he says. With a snap of his fingers the

Knights follow in the Mitchell's direction with Reed at the front of the lineup. My eyes scan the crowd as all eyes turn to us. Wankstein nods her head in approval.

"This shit is freaking me the fuck out," Frost rumbles against my ear, and I bark out a laugh. I turn my head so our noses are touching.

"Get used to it," I sass with a smirk. He growls pulling me closer.

"You ready for a happily ever after Bo-Bo?" he asks with a dark chuckle. My eyes scan the area, and the student body nod their heads in acknowledgement of what's happened here today. They know now what will happen if they go too far, and from the looks on their faces – I don't think they're going to cause us any problems anytime soon. My eyes land on the guys next. Pride and lust shine on their faces making my cheeks heat. Frost's and my eyes connect, and the iridescent blue has me wanting to get lost in their depths.

"Yeah, I think I am."

ABOUT THE AUTHOR

Tatum is a mum of two girls, while also being a writer, Netflix and coffee addict. She loves to write dark stories with both why choose and MF romances that will take you on one hell of an emotional rollercoaster. Characters that will have you blowing so hot and cold you won't know how to feel at any given time and who love to shatter your heart. Does she laugh while she puts the shards back together? Maybe just a little bit.

Visit her online:
www.tatumrayneauthor.com

or join the Trouble Makers or newsletter on website to stay up to date.
You can find the reader group here: https://www.facebook.com/groups/tatumraynesreadergroup/?ref=share_group_link

ALSO BY TATUM RAYNE

BROAD CREEK PREP

(Dark, Academy, MF Romance)

Broken Prince

BLACK FROST ACADEMY DUET

(Dark, Bully, College-age Academy, Why choose Romance)

Black Frost Academy

Return to Black Frost Academy

THE DAMNED CREW

(Dark, Mafia MF Romance)

Ruthless Monsters

OTHER AUTHORS AT HUDSON INDIE INK

Paranormal Romance/Urban Fantasy

Stephanie Hudson

Xen Randell

C. L. Monaghan

Sorcha Dawn

Harper Phoenix

Sci-fi/Fantasy

Devin Hanson

Crime/Action

Blake Hudson

Jack Walker

Contemporary Romance

Gemma Weir

Nikki Ashton

Anna Bloom

Tatum Rayne

9 781916 562066